The Woodcutter's House

The

Woodcutter's House

By

Robert Nathan 1894 –

❧

The Bobbs-Merrill Company

Publishers   *Indianapolis*

TO
My Friend
BEN GRUNTAL

CONTENTS

The Woodcutter's House

The Woodcutter's House

CHAPTER 1

THE ROAD UP HEMLOCK

THAT was the spring poor Ezra Adams died. Trembling and meek, he stepped into Jordan's dark icy water, the cold tide froze him, and he came out again in Zion with a look of peace; he seemed to be saying humbly to the angels, "I don't amount to much, but I feel friendly."

He forgot the home he had left, the small bare shack on public ground at the village edge, the cheerless faces of his neighbors, the preacher's last grave words, uttered without much hope; he forgot his poverty and his pain, and he forgot his daughter Metabel, baptized Mehitabel, to whom he left his bedding, an old hammer, a corncob pipe, some pans for cooking, and a broken chair. She was his only friend; he hated to leave her alone in the world, and died, as he said, regretful. Two days later, in the evening, he was buried.

At that time Metabel was sixteen-going-on-seventeen, small for her age, with rain-colored eyes. Her thrush-colored hair was tied in a knot at the back of her head; and her shoes had holes in them. She did not pity herself, but she felt lonely. Early the next day, she went slowly out of the house and up the hill to the place she loved, a little clearing on the slope above Barly, where she could see Old Hemlock in the distance. The dawn was just breaking; it was too early for birds, too early even for shadows. The trees stood up dark and still in the air cold as water. Metabel drew her shawl around her, and sat down; and

Musket, the fiddler's little dog, who had been with her all that night, sat down too, and put his nose in her hand.

Metabel had a lot to think about. In the first place, her pa was dead; he'd forgot her, he'd gone off in the dark, out of sight, out of call . . . gone off over Jordan River. Oh, Jordan River . . . everyday thoughts couldn't get across it. And if you took all your heart and all your loneliness, and went crying out over it, it didn't help you any; as far as you could get, there was only the dark and the empty water. Nobody answered.

Far away, far as the moon, and around curves you couldn't see . . . she didn't pity herself, it was her pa she pitied, all alone in the icy dark with no one to look out for him. Her heart trembled with woe; poor pa . . .

"O Lord," she prayed devoutly, "look after him, he's so meek."

And she added in despair, "Don't leave him all alone by himself."

She sat huddled in her shawl, staring out across the dawn-gray meadows from which the mists of night still rose like the smoke of leaves, uneasy, blown by the wind.

She needed some one to look after, to do for, as she had done all her life for her pa. It was a matter of affection with her, a shy, maternal kindness: she was like a little dreamy mother, with no one to bring up.

And now that he was gone, the loneliness she felt was more for her pa than for herself; she saw him lost and frightened on the road to Heaven, and ached for him.

She knew what they were saying about her in the village; she could almost hear them. There was the preacher: he'd want her to have a good home. and stop dancing in the

woods and meadows above Barly. He'd want
her to dance like the others in barns decorated
with pumpkins or first spring flowers; he'd
want her to live with a good woman, and be
taken care of. That was the way a girl ought
to live, under a proper wing.

They'd all want her under a wing now, she
thought, they'd want to look after her, to tell
her not to do this, and not to do that. Even
the fiddler and his wife—there wasn't much
they'd likely disallow her, but on the other
hand she'd be of no advantage to them, seeing
they looked after each other. And there wasn't
any one else in Barly who'd want to take her,
except to disallow her; no one wanted her,
really, with her shy way of smiling like one
who rarely got it back again, and her way of
dancing all alone in the woods, which some
held queer, and others sinful.

Her hand tightened over Musket's nose.

"Who'd ever want me," she said, "unless to change me over?"

And for the first time her eyes filled with tears, not at being left alone, but at being changed over.

The little dog's heart was heavy, but at the same time he did not let his grief for Metabel get the better of him. If Metabel was affectionate, Musket was practical; it was his nature to be tidy and able, to see what there was, and not to tell himself stories. As he sat beside her, with his nose in her hand, he thought to himself, "Probably this is the end of our good times together." But because her fingers hurt him, he moved away, just a little, as though to say, "Excuse me, I am uncomfortable."

Musket had been a dancer in his youth. When he lived with the fiddler, he used to hop about on his hind legs, one, two, one two three; and collect coins in a hat held in his mouth. The fiddler used to say to him, "Musket, you dance in order to live. Nevertheless, I believe that you like to be admired."

And he would add with a smile, "Musket, you are a humbug."

But that was long ago, when they were both younger. Now the little dog liked nothing better than to watch Metabel skipping about, her hair flying, and her arms stuck out like the branches of a tree. Too old any longer to dance, he liked to remember that he had also been an artist, in a manner of speaking, and could tell what was good from what was bad.

However, he was of no use to Metabel in this emergency. His tail went thump against the ground, but that was all; he had nothing to suggest. As a matter of fact, Metabel was not paying any attention to him. She sat looking with cloudy eyes across the valleys of her home, to where the night-blue hills already caught the light. The air was fresh, the valleys were dark and still; only in the north, far off, the clear day shone like a fire on the hills. She took a deep breath.

"Musket," she said, "there's the sun.

"It's day on Hemlock."

With hungry eyes she watched the light steal downward on the mountain. There it was day, while she still sat in shadow. Queer, how it made her feel to see; as though life, somehow, were different there on Hemlock, where the rocks and trees shone so brightly in the sun—as though life were freer and kinder in that gleaming air than down in the valley with the preacher and the Watsons and the Lowerees.

"If I were up there now," she thought, "I'd hold out my arms like this. . . ."

Musket moved aside; he thought she was going to dance. Her thin little body lifted itself with longing toward the hills; the day seemed to make things better for pa, it couldn't be cold and dark for him with that clear light shining there on Hemlock. . . .

"That's where my friends are," she said.

She had no friends, except the fiddler and his wife, in the whole world. But she felt as though up there on Hemlock she had friends; as though beyond those fields which nursed the Barly cows, beyond that strip of woods, beyond that rise and valley to the north, in cleaner, sweeter air, in brighter, kinder light, her how-do-you-do would not be left unanswered, her small shy smile be given back again.

It wouldn't be in Barly, that was sure— not by the folks who knew her, and held her no-account. All her life she'd just missed be-

19

ing said how-do-you-do to; she didn't mind, so long as there was pa to look after. But now that he was gone, and there was no one for her to do for, she'd be looked after herself by somebody else; she wouldn't be free any more—free to tell herself stories, free to dance in the woods like a piece of wind, or a little goat—no, not any more; she'd be brought into the fold with the sheep, and driven along the straight high road to Heaven in company with the Watsons and the Lowerees.

And she didn't want to be; she wanted to go after her pa, to do the simple, kindly things for him she'd always done. Her gray eyes ached with it, she wanted it so much.

"Musket dear," she said, "don't look if I cry, will you."

But she didn't cry; the light on Hemlock filled her eyes, instead. It seemed to her as though that were the way he must have gone,

up past Hemlock, out beyond the hills . . .
not through the dark any more, or around
curves you couldn't see, but straight out,
through the light. . . .

She stood up, as tall as she was able. "Musket," she said, "I'm going up on Hemlock."

And with her old blue shawl around her, she
started out. "We'll be there by noon," she
said.

CHAPTER 2

"THERE'S NO ROAD OVER HEMLOCK"

MUSKET walked along without enthusiasm; his mind was a prey to forebodings, and he gazed at the ground with a gloomy expression. He did not expect any good to come of this excursion; at the very least, it was a long walk up, and a long walk back. "A hill is never anything when you get to it," he said; "all you see is other hills, which look grander than the one you are on. What I say is, if you wish to look up at a hill, then stay down in the valley where you can see it."

He addressed these remarks to a young May-bug. But the May-bug did not agree with him.

22

"You are old," she said; "that is the trouble. You sound very wise, but the truth of the matter is you do not feel anything. Any one can be a philosopher, in that case. It is quite another matter with me. An emotion I cannot control fills me with the liveliest joy. Hope lifts my wings. Perhaps by to-morrow I shall be a mother. What an exciting life."

And she flew away, into a spider web. "Even if I am not to be a mother," she murmured, as the spider began to eat her; "I am entirely too young to be a philosopher."

"Musket," said Metabel, looking back, "we'll be there by afternoon."

But Musket did not believe her. With his tail between his legs and his nose to the ground, he trudged along, through the sweet-smelling, early spring morning. The little white butterflies danced in the sunshine without attracting his attention; the young green grasshoppers leapt full of joy and vigor into the air. And Metabel walked eagerly forward, her gray eyes lifted to the morning sky, the spring's deep blue, blue as the sea.

All about her the tiny voices of earth sang her their little songs of consolation. The first flute of birds in the branches, the early hum of bees, the tree-toad's bell, spoke to her heart, lonely and loving. "Metabel," they said, "are you looking for some one you loved? He is not far away, he has slipped into the shadow of a leaf, he has stolen into the silence after birdsong. Can you tell, my child, where birdsong ends, and silence begins? Perhaps, if your ears are sharp, you will hear him again; perhaps you will see him, if your eyes are clear, over your shoulder like the faint new moon.

"Do not be lonely, little sister, do not think

you have no one to love any more. There is still the earth to love, where clover and daisies grow, where the bees fly with golden legs. And he is there, with last year's song of birds, with next year's bloom of rose. They are not very far, they are just out of sight. . . . There, you have missed them.

"Look again, little cousin."

The sun rode higher and higher in the sky, the fresh clear air of the spring morning gave way to the warm fragrance of noon. From the valleys, as the road ascended, there swam up to her through the sunny atmosphere the moist odors of earth and dung, the barnyard smell of cows; from the woods came out to her the hot sweet scent of balsam. A flight of crows rose from a field with noontime cries, a robin sang in a tree, three notes like water falling, and then was still to listen.

"Musket," she said, "it smells so good.

25

"We'll be there soon." And she gave him a little pat, to reassure him.

But Hemlock was further away than she thought. The sun went down again in the slow spring way, the shadows lengthened little by little to the east; and still the mountain was before her and above her. Slowly the light drew away into the south, the sky over Hemlock grew colder and darker. Was she going the wrong way? She stopped and looked about her. She was far from home, and hungry. What had made her walk so far, she wondered; and where was she?

She was a good many miles north of Barly, she knew that. And as for what had brought her . . . did she hope to find her pa again on that dark lonely hill? Oh no—her pa was dead.

She sat down suddenly by the side of the road. And Musket, anxious and depressed, sat wearily down beside her, and leaned his head against her knee. The shadows lengthened to the east, the sun drew closer to the tree-tops.

It was the lonely hour before dusk, when the sun has no warmth, and the heart grows weary. The sparkle was gone from the air, the little voices of earth were quiet and remote. Soon the light would deepen into blue, soft as a faded cornflower. Then it would be time to go home.

Home?

"We're a long ways from home," said Metabel, and her head drooped. "We're a long ways from supper," she said.

The misty sad spring evening settled down. The frogs began to shrill, a dog barked far away. And Metabel, with a long sigh to keep her chin from trembling, turned her face home.

But this time Musket led the way. The little dog, hungry and dejected, had only one idea, to find his supper as soon as possible. He was tired of walking up and down hills, from which, as he said, it was useless to expect anything. The practical thing was to get home again, or to find, at least, a house with a fire in it, and some one to give them supper. For this reason when, at a turn of the road, he smelled bacon on the right, to the right he went, Barly or no Barly; and Metabel, lost and weary, followed him without thinking.

It was like night under the trees, it was hard to see; the road was narrow, and no more than a path. She went along in a numb way, her feet following Musket, her mind in a cloud; branches whipped at her out of the darkness, roots lay tangled about like snakes under her feet. Presently one tripped her; she

28

caught her foot in a hemlock root, and down she went, thump.

It knocked the dreamy misery out of her, along with the wind. "Musket," she said with a gasp, "wherever are we going?"

But Musket was on ahead. There was nothing to do but follow him, or else sit where she was. She got to her feet, and went forward slowly, feeling for roots with her toes. There seemed an uncommon number of them . . . were they really roots? . . . and not snakes or hairy fingers?

"Musket dear," she said in a shaky voice, "where are you?"

But just as she was ready to feel scary, she caught a glimpse of lantern light at the end of the path. There, between the trees, she spied a low cottage; and in the warm light at the door stood Musket, gazing inside with anxious cheer, while the owners, a young man and an old one, gazed amiably out.

"Come in," they said.

With shy, friendly looks they offered her a chair. It was a rocker, with only one arm, and half the back gone. She sat down in it, and, closing her eyes, held out her feet to the fire. The chair squeaked as she rocked up and down. She was so tired, so hungry and sleepy; it was warm in front of the fire, it was like lying out in a clover field on a sunny day. She rocked up and down, squeak, squeak. . . .

They gave her hot milk to drink, bread and butter, soup, and apple pie. Then when she felt better they asked her questions. They looked at her with awkward smiles, and she looked back at them gravely, out of her rain-gray eyes. The old one made her think of pa; he had no coat, he wore an old red flannel

30

undershirt, and his suspenders were made out of string. The young one wore overalls; they smelled of fresh-cut wood. His eyes were dark—black almost. . . .

"Black as little roots," she thought drowsily, "black as old acorns."

Squeak, squeak. . . .

When she told them she'd come from Barly, they shook their heads, and looked queer. It turned out they'd never heard of it, although she knew it was just down the road a piece. But no, they'd never heard of Barly, neither of them. "And we've lived here, man and boy, all our lives," said the old man.

"There's Lander's Center," he continued, "and the Mill Junction. And Wayne, down the road, and Farmingdale. And there's Green Center, and East Toby. . . . But Barly? No, ma'am, there's no Barly, no Barly whatsoever."

"That's where my friends are, Barly," said Metabel dreamily.

The young man scratched his head with a thoughtful air. He, too, had never heard of Barly. Wayne was down the road a piece; up the road was nothing at all. "The road," he said, "goes down, but it don't go up. It stops here. There's no road over Hemlock. There's no road whatever."

"You're lost, ma'am," said the old one; "lost for fair."

"Maybe," said the young one. . . .

"Maybe nothing," said the old one, who knew his own mind. "There's no such place as Barly," he said.

And they both stood looking down at Metabel, who had come from Barly, or from the moon, what was the difference?

She was too tired to argue about it. In the morning she'd find the road again, and go home. Musket lay at her feet, blinking into the fire. There must be Barly somewhere, because there was Musket. . . . Her head drooped, her eyes closed. The last thing she saw was a red flannel undershirt; the young man had eyes like black susanflowers. Clover in a field, the warm sun . . . daisies, black-eyed susans, dancing in the sun. . . .

Squeak.

They brought a mattress in, and laid her on it, covered by a blanket. Then they went to bed. The young one slept on the bare boards, because it was his mattress on which Metabel lay sleeping.

CHAPTER 3

METABEL DECIDES TO STAY

THEY were right; the road before the house was not the road she'd come on; there was no road back to Barly. She found that out for herself the next morning, after she'd walked about in the woods upwards of an hour looking for it, only to find herself back at the house again. The old man in the red flannel undershirt was sitting on the door-step; he smiled when he saw her.

"Excuse me," she said humbly; "I'm lost."

It didn't surprise him any. "You are," he agreed, "you are. I knew it from the first. 'Joseph,' I said to my nephew—he being named Joseph—'the girl's lost.' And what did he say to me? 'Maybe,' he said. 'Maybe nothing,' I said. Barly—go along."

And spitting heartily into the grass, he gazed at her with satisfaction.

Metabel and Musket stood before him in the sunlight, small and dejected. "What am I to do?" she asked. "Maybe if I went down to Wayne, or East Toby, I could get home that way. But Wayne's way the other side of Hemlock from Barly. So how would I get there?"

"You're in Wayne now," said the old man. "Leastways, you're on Hemlock. Wayne village is down the road a piece. Hemlock peak is about a mile behind you. I don't rightly know how you got here from over the other side. But being as you're here, I've no objection. Have a bite of breakfast with us. Joseph's putting on the coffee now."

"Thank you," she said.

"Well," he added, not unkindly, "a bite won't hurt us any."

But a sudden thought made him pause. "I expect your folks will be uneasy," he said.

"I have no folks," she answered. "My pa is dead. Pa was all the folks I had, beyond Musket here."

"Oh," said he. And he said again, more kindly, "Come in and have your bite with us."

Seen in the morning light, the nephew Joseph was not a handsome man. He was shy, but he was friendly; he said little, and contented himself with smiling at Metabel over the top of his saucer out of which he drank his coffee. Metabel stared back at him with surprise; she wasn't used to having folks smile at her for no reason; it made her feel fluttery.

But the old man did most of the talking.

"Right behind you," he said, "is the tallest hill in the county. I figure that makes us the highest farm in this section; we're two thousand three hundred and forty feet up. Still, we don't get much company up here.

"My nephew," he went on, "is a woodcutter. Not a very good one, neither. Well, I must tell you, that's a grief to me. I do a little farming myself; I raise the biggest heads of lettuce in the county."

"My Uncle Henry," said Joseph proudly, "is a power with vegetables."

"Well, that's so," said Uncle Henry. However, very soon he began to look gloomy and dissatisfied. "This is a small county," he observed. "I could do with a bigger."

"It's enough for me," said Joseph cheerfully.

"You're too easy satisfied," remarked his uncle.

"That's so," said Joseph, and relapsed into silence.

"We don't have much company up here," said Uncle Henry, "that's a fact." He rubbed his chin, and looked at Metabel with a gleam of hope. "How would you like to see where I've put my lettuce?" he asked.

"I'd like it fine," said Metabel. "Let me clean up first, and I'll go right along with you."

She went over to the sink, and got a foamy suds going. "She uses a power of soap," said Uncle Henry, "it's a right unusual sight."

"It is," said Joseph. And he went off to the barn, where he kept his tools. Soon the sound of his axe could be heard in the woods near by, metallic and clear.

When the dishes were dried, Uncle Henry took Metabel around to look at the lettuces. There was nothing to be seen; it was too early. "Here's where they're going to be," he said; "the biggest heads in Wayne County."

And he stood gazing with pride at the bare brown earth, raked and combed to let the young green lettuce through.

He took her to see the coop he'd made for the hens, the oak handle Joseph had whittled for the pump, the south field near the road where he had planted his corn. They went to the barn to see Isaiah, the meek gray horse, who was near as old as Joseph, he said, but more use. She liked Isaiah, she put her thin hand out to feel his nose; he had Musket's way of looking at a body, so sober and true. The morning was half over before they started back to the house again.

"I ought to be getting on," said Metabel. Wherever Barly was, it was a long way off.

But Uncle Henry was in no hurry to have her go. "Take your bite of dinner with us," he said; "another bite won't hurt us, either."

It didn't take much urging for her to say

she would. But when Joseph made to cook it, she took the pots out of his hands. She felt at home, and quite happy. "Do you like Indian pudding?" she asked. "I'll put some on for your supper.

"Go on out, and set a while. I'll call you when I'm ready."

She went out to get herself a bowl of dandelions for the table. The spring sun shone down on her, the moist earth gave out a sweet mist of smells. Over in the field behind the house, where the woods ended, Musket was talking to the old gray horse; they regarded each other earnestly, exchanging profound looks. A robin hopped out on the grass among the dandelions; behind her in the woods she heard a chipmunk scold. "Am I really over Hemlock," she wondered. Startled, she looked around at the air, to see if it looked higher.

When she was ready, she called them in.

"Look here," said Uncle Henry, "there's flowers on the table." And he added with his mouth full,

"This is the best cooked beans I ever eat.

"Mind how these beans taste, Joseph."

Joseph said nothing; when dinner was over he went back to his woodchopping, and left Metabel to do the dishes. Uncle Henry pushed away his empty plate with a sigh. He drew the back of his hand across his mouth, and pulled at the strings which held up his trousers. "A fine day," he declared.

"Isn't it," said Metabel happily.

"It's misty in the valley," said Uncle Henry. "You wouldn't get a day like this lower down."

"I guess you wouldn't either," she agreed.

"No," he said, "you wouldn't."

He was silent, thinking. "Just the same," he remarked finally, "we don't get much company up here."

And he added, almost shyly, "What for do you want to hurry home?"

In the afternoon silence she went about the house putting things in order. She had nothing else to do, and no way, as far as she could see, of going anywhere. She'd have to start early in the morning to get back to Barly at all. Meanwhile there was plenty to do in the cottage: a corner or two to sweep out, dishes to arrange in the cupboard, a dishcloth to wash; before she knew it, it was time to put the supper on. The stove gave out a ruddy glow, it shone in her eyes and on her pink cheeks; she brushed a wisp of hair back from her forehead, and poured out the Indian pudding.

Supper was eaten in silence. Even Uncle Henry had nothing to say; he sighed happily over the pudding, but beyond that, nothing. He seemed to be tiptoeing about in his mind, as though a thought were up there he was half afraid of: he wanted it there, but feared to scare it off by going at it. As for Metabel, she was used to silence; she'd spoken mostly when she was spoken to all her life, it didn't trouble her any. But when the dishes were put away and the mattress brought out again, Uncle Henry spoke.

"Joseph," he said, "her pa's dead."

"I'm sorry to hear it," said Joseph.

"Yes," said Uncle Henry, "she has no pa. What she's got she says is in Barly."

"That's queer," said Joseph.

Uncle Henry was creeping up on his thought; he was trying to take it unaware. "Barly," he said, "that's a good long ways."

"Where would it be?" asked Joseph.

"Ah," said Uncle Henry, "where?"

Taking up the lamp, he turned to Metabel. "Sleep tight," he said. And then in a whisper, hoarse and hearty, he added, "Stay as long as you're minded to. . . ."

It was close enough; he shut the door with pride.

"Good night," said Metabel. "Good night. . . .

"Good night, Joseph."

She lay down on her mattress, with Musket beside her; the little dog felt her thin arm around him, tight and loving. "Musket," she whispered, "do you think they want us to stay? I think maybe they do. . . . Anyhow we haven't anywhere else to go. Just suppose there wasn't any Barly . . . what would we do?

"You haven't any friends here, have you? But there's Isaiah. I haven't any friends anywhere.

"Go to sleep, Musket dear. Go to sleep now. . . ."

44

CHAPTER 4

IN WHICH MUSKET MEETS A WASP

So METABEL stayed, and did the cooking and cleaning and mending for Joseph and Uncle Henry. The mountain spring bloomed and blossomed, and Metabel's heart blossomed with it. Even with pa she'd never been so happy, never had so much she liked to do; the little shack outside Barly was bare and ugly compared to the cottage on Hemlock, where the pines stood up dark against the sky, and the dogwood opened like lilies in the wood. The clear warm air brought color to her cheeks; from having lived all her life on an egg borrowed here and a loaf of bread there, she found herself for the first time with more

45

than she could eat. They made a bed for her
in the attic; the high narrow room was full of
old apples and dried wasps' nests, as sweet a
smelling place to sleep, she thought, as ever
she'd seen. She still had Joseph's mattress; he
allowed he'd sleep on balsam until winter.

But if Metabel was happy, Uncle Henry
was happier still. To be sure, it gave him Indian pudding, but what was more important,
it gave him some one to talk to. The tiny
parade of his own life seemed to him to call
for comment: to be, in a manner of speaking,
an argument between himself and oblivion.
Obstinate, but anxious, he longed to hear that
what with one thing and another, between the
strength of his opinions and the size of his
lettuces, the debate was not altogether lost.

He was the champion lettuce raiser of
Wayne County, but he had further ambitions.
His own size seemed to him, in a mystical but

46

natural way, to be as big as his lettuces. He longed to excel in cubic content; he wished in his heart to raise the biggest lettuce in the whole state, or in the world. He never spoke of it, but when he thought there might be bigger lettuces somewhere else, he grew very gloomy.

And it was, as he sometimes said to Metabel, a grief to him to think that Joseph was no more than a moderate woodchopper. "What beats me," he said, "is how he can be so no-account, and so content." He admitted that Joseph was neat with an axe; it was the lack of size in his work which bothered him. "He cuts wood," he said, "like it didn't matter. I've seen him squat down in front of a tree a whole morning, before he'd so much as lift an axe to it—studying out how to make it fall neat. Sometimes he won't even take a tree at all; the mountain's full of ash, but he won't take it. Don't care to, he says, though there's a price for ash at the mill. Just tell me what's the sense in that?"

Metabel smiled; it reminded her a little bit of pa—not much, not the neatness part, but the no-account part, the don't-care-to part. "Maybe he's got something on his mind," she said, "besides woodcutting."

"Then what for does he cut wood?" asked Uncle Henry simply. "Taking it just the way it suits him—that's not woodcutting proper. I don't know what it is."

Whatever it was, woodcutting or not woodcutting, it didn't seem to bother Joseph any. He remained quiet and friendly, shy, but without anxiety. She heard his axe like a clear bell in the woods, followed by long silences; sometimes there was a rush and thunder of sound as a tree fell—neatly, she expected, leaving the forest orderly. At meals he smiled at her across

48

the rim of his saucer, or over his plate; he had little to say, mostly to agree with his uncle, or to express a mild joy and wonder. He was a happy man, with nothing so far as she could see, to be happy about—what made him so happy, she wondered? In her own case it was doing things for people, being liked or admired, maybe loved, even—but who admired Joseph? Not his Uncle Henry, at any rate.

Still, there it was: without being admired, he was a happy man, at least to look at. It had a way of making her feel happy too. She took to dancing, when she thought no one was looking, and sang herself little songs. Her young voice, thin and sweet-and-sour, rose from the kitchen in lively hymns out of Barly Church, or dancing tunes she'd heard the fiddler play. Uncle Henry, in the lettuce-bed, listened without objection. It didn't amount

to much, her singing, but he didn't mind, seeing she enjoyed it.

"Musket," she said, "do you think Joseph
is no-account? He puts me in mind of pa; he
takes his time, and he doesn't care. Pa was
no-account for fair, but I loved him. He never
got anything done, mostly. He just set still
and thought about things. And I did for him."

She added with a serious sigh, "I wouldn't
have changed so much as a mouse's tail on
him."

Musket did not discuss these things with
Metabel. He preferred to exchange his opinions with the horse Isaiah, in whose mild dark
eyes shone the drowned lights of patience and
reflection.

He found Isaiah at the south end of the
pasture; with his head resting on the pasture
bars, the old gray horse was gazing, motion-
less, into space. Dazzled by his friend's pow-

erful body and enigmatic expression, Musket
remained respectfully silent. At last he said,

"It is always the distance which is most
attractive. However, when one gets there, one
turns around and looks back, because in that
direction, also, is distance. What is the use
of looking for something which cannot be
found? I believe in being satisfied with what
one has, and not traveling too much. If we
had stayed home, we should still be in Barly,
with the fiddler and Mrs. Sebold, and the
rooster Bartholomew."

"Are you homesick?" asked Isaiah kindly.

"Why should I be homesick?" replied Musket; "wherever I go, my home is under Metabel's bed. No, I was simply speaking from a
philosophical point of view. . . . Well, just
tell me, what is the good of it? These lettuces
for example—suppose they are bigger and
bigger? There is no end to that sort of thing."

Isaiah gave his head an indulgent shake. "My poor friend," he said, "you have led a very dissipated life. You have been a dancer; I do not object to dancing, but it is not the same thing as pulling logs to town. You do not know what it is to work; you do not know what it is to go to bed so tired that your bones ache. What happiness; it is the only happiness in the world worth talking about."

Musket gave a shudder. "I have been cold," he said, "and I have gone hungry to bed many times with legs worn out with dancing. I suppose you think an artist's life is all pleasure. You are mistaken: and going to bed alone is not what I like to think about."

"To go to bed alone," said Isaiah, "is the only way I would ever wish to go. I stretch myself out, I think of all the things I have done during the day. . . . That is better than dancing around in a meadow. To work, and to respect the work of others . . . that is a natural and noble life. But I can see that you are a cynic and do not respect anything."

"I am not a cynic," said Musket earnestly; "I simply say there is something else. . . . What is the good of working so hard, when all the rest of the world is playing, when the flowers are blooming, and the little yellow butterflies are dancing together? Why not be happy where we are, and also dance a little because the sky is so blue, or because our hearts are light? To laugh, to cry . . . what does it matter? To feel—that is the thing; and it is better to feel happy than to feel sad, in my opinion."

"I do not feel sad," replied Isaiah; "I work too hard, I have no time to feel sad. What an emotional creature you are. That is because you do nothing all the time. I should go crazy with such a life." And he stamped his foot on

53

the ground, to embarrass some flies who were biting him.

After a while he said in a friendlier tone, "I believe you are living in the attic. That is where the apples are kept." And he added with a thoughtful air, "It is a long time since I have tasted a good apple."

"Allow me to get you one," said Musket, turning politely toward the house.

Isaiah called after him, "One is probably all you can carry. But if it is small, perhaps you would have room for two."

When Musket arrived in the attic, he started to take a large greening in his mouth, to bring to Isaiah. But just then a wasp crawled around from the other side of it, and gave him a gloomy look. "What is all this?" asked the wasp. "What are you doing with my apple?"

"Excuse me," said Musket hastily. "I was

54

simply going to take some fruit to Isaiah. . . .
However, if it is your apple, I wouldn't dream
. . . there is another one over there which
will do just as well."

"That is also my apple," said the wasp. "In
fact," he added, "these are all my apples. I
am the largest apple-owning wasp in this county. Do you think I have spent my entire life
watching these treasures in order to have you
give them away to your friends? Do not be so
foolish as to imagine it." And he lifted his
slender waist with an ominous sound.

Musket went quickly backwards. "Forgive
me," he said politely; "I had no idea of it.
And Isaiah—I am sure when he realizes how
hard you have worked over these apples, he
will be the very last one in the world to wish to
eat one."

So saying, he returned to the meadow without the apple. But when he told Isaiah what

had happened, the old horse's eyes snapped with rage. "What a little fool you are," he said to him angrily; "you might just as well say that this grass belongs to me. You should simply have taken the apple, and come down here with it."

This speech, which he did not expect, caused Musket to grow very thoughtful. He replied stiffly to Isaiah, "You must not expect a dancer to know what belongs to each person, and what does not. Please remember that the wasp was very much in earnest; I have never seen a more serious wasp. . . . Besides, naturally I thought you would wish to respect the work he had done, on which he told me that he had spent his entire life. . . ."

Isaiah said nothing; putting his head down, he began to crop the sweet green grass, through which tiny insects hurried with cries of fright and pain to get out of his way.

CHAPTER 5

AND METABEL MEETS THE LITTLE GREEN MAN

METABEL had taken a pail of milk to Joseph in the woods, in case he was thirsty. They stood together by a giant pine whose straight dark trunk rose beyond tiptoe reach before it broke into branches. "There's a tree," said Metabel dreamily; "look, Joseph, the way it goes up and up, like a noble king. What does it make you think of?"

"Neat cut wood," said Joseph simply.

"Oh," said Metabel. She looked up at it with pursed lips. Yes, she could see it that way, too . . . just neat cut wood. Poor tree.

All at once Joseph had a lot to say. "That tree," he declared, "says to me, 'You can't cut me down as neat as I can stand here.' " And swinging his axe in a bright circle, he drove the blade into the dark trunk, which shivered with the impact.

"But I wouldn't cut an ash," he said, "not for anything.

"I like to see them grow."

Metabel turned away; it made her dizzy to see trees come down; they came down with such a bump from so high up. "Bring me home some knots for the stove," she said, "and some bark for the smell. . . ."

She went down through the woods toward the house. The light fell green and yellow through the leaves, birds sang in the branches. A small red squirrel scampered up a birch, flirted himself out through the leaves, and leaped with tiny, outstretched claws into another tree; the slim twig bent as he fled along the branch, noisy as a waterfall, light as a puff of wind. Underfoot the sapling roots pushed up through the dead pine needles; somewhere water sang in the woods, dropped and tinkled. She raised her arms above her head and danced a few steps down the red pine needles and the moss; she remembered the way she used to dance when she was a child . . . this is the way the wind dances, this is the way a rabbit goes, hop, hop. . . .

And with her arms still over her head, hop she went, right into a little man dressed in green, who was sitting under a wild rose bush, quietly talking to some mice.

"Oh," she said, and stood stock-still, as though, all at once, some one had laid a finger on her heart.

The little green man paid no attention to her; he went on addressing the mice, who listened to him with anxious looks. "My poor friends," he said to them, "it is just as important for snakes to have mice to eat, as it is for mice not to have snakes to eat them. Do you expect me to alter the designs of nature? Go away, please; and if you have to be eaten, do not feel that it is a personal reflection on you in any way."

The mice ran away like black drops of water; sighing, their instructor looked up at Metabel, and shook his head. "Ak," he said, "the little anxious mice."

"I'd be anxious too," said Metabel, "if I were mice."

At this his face took on a more serious expression. "If one must be a mouse," he said, "one may as well be cheerful, and accept it as an accident of nature. The gods cannot change these things, least of all a small god, like me."

Metabel looked at him gravely; in the dim forest light he seemed to her no bigger than she was herself. "I knew you were something queer," she said, "the minute I laid eyes on you. But you don't look like God very much—not the one we had in Barly. I used to see Him in the Bible over to the Widow Sebold's, with a long white beard."

The little green man smiled at her—a friendlier smile, she thought, than any she had ever seen, friendlier than Joseph's even, though it reminded her of Joseph's. "I've never been in Barly," he said; "there is no one there for me to visit. I live up here, on Hemlock, because Joseph lives here. I am very fond of Joseph. He is all I have to be fond of, so far as I can see."

And he added sadly, "I am a very small god."

"Yes, you are," said Metabel critically. And she added at once, for fear she had offended him, "Excuse me."

He looked at her doubtfully, with his head
to one side, like a robin. "Did I say I cared?"
he demanded. "I do not care at all. I have a
very good time. During the day I walk up
and down in these quiet woods, and watch
Joseph chop down trees. How he handles his
axe—never too much, just enough. . . .

"Still," he added thoughtfully, "one or two
more to be fond of would not do me any
harm—if only to have something to fall back
on in an emergency.

"Supposing I were to lose him?"

And he gave a shudder to think of it.

Her hands clasped, her head bent, Metabel
stood before him in the green spring woods;
the sun shone in her thrush-colored hair, shadows of leaves floated up and down on her cal-
ico dress. "Why are you fond of Joseph?" she
asked. "And why haven't you any one else to
be fond of?"

62

The little man waved his hand in the air. "I am fond of him," he said simply, "for the same reason that you are."

"I'm not," said Metabel with surprise.

"I admire him," he continued, "for his good humor. As a matter of fact, that is what I am god of." And he added sturdily, "I am small, but I am unique.

"As for there being any one else to be fond of, that is not something one can pick up anywhere. . . . You were dancing a moment ago with your hands over your head, looking very awkward, but happy. Shall I be fond of you? You are small, too, but lively."

However, Metabel was not paying any attention to what he was saying: she was thinking about Joseph. "You don't think he's trifling?" she asked doubtfully.

The little man drooped; he seemed to grow smaller still. "What," he exclaimed, "do you

want him to be a successful woodchopper?
Dear me!

"In that case, I do not think I shall be fond
of you at all."

"Nobody asked you to," said Metabel. And
she added, with red cheeks, "I don't want him
to be anything whatever.

"What do I care what he is?" she whispered.

"Oh," said the little man; "ah. Nevertheless, you think about him a great deal. And
you have even sewed up that hole in your
stocking, just above the knee, which might
never be seen, but suppose you fell down?"

"Well," said Metabel with a gasp.

The little man wagged a finger at her.
"Now you are red as a rose," he declared; "but
do not lose your temper."

"Why should I lose my temper," said Metabel loftily, "just because you're so rude and
silly?"

The little green man drew himself up, not without dignity. "Your remarks cannot shake my divine good humor;" he said, "because for one thing, I am not obliged to listen to them."

So saying, he made her a polite bow, and went off through the woods, humming a song to himself. Metabel stood still, looking after him with stormy eyes.

"Just the same," she said, but too low for him to hear, "I don't think you're very nice."

And she went home without dancing, to pick some spinach for supper.

CHAPTER 6

TWELVE DOZEN JAMS AND JELLIES

SHE was mending Joseph's socks when Uncle Henry called for her with Isaiah, to take her to town. They went down in the farm wagon; she sat up in front with Uncle Henry, while Musket crouched at her feet and gazed appreciatively at Isaiah's hind-quarters rising and falling as he trotted. "Ah," he thought to himself, "now he is working; this is what he enjoys. I feel a profound respect for him. I would not like to do it myself, but viewed from here, it is heroic." And curling himself up, he lay down against the dashboard, comforted by the thought of Isaiah's sober excellence.

"What's Wayne like, Uncle Henry?" asked

Metabel. Her eager eyes explored the road as it wound down the mountain. She saw the birches on the lower slopes, she saw the stony fields full of berry bushes; they looked sunny and strange to her, seen for the first time from the seat of a wagon owned by a family to which, even ever so little, she belonged.

Uncle Henry gave a swish of his whip at the trees. "I allow it's not a very big place," he said, "that is, looking at it from a sizable point of view. There's a church there, as neat a piece of God's house as any in the county. And we've got the county bank.

"Yes, ma'am," he said, "we've got the county bank."

It seemed to afford him unusual relish; and he went on to talk about it. St. John Deakan owned it, but his daughter Prissy helped him. St. John was a wealthy man, he owned Deakan's Saw Mill as well, but Prissy was the real success. She was not exactly young any more, as young people went, but she handled a great deal of money. A smart woman, was Uncle Henry's opinion of her, with a power of success in her. Likely she could make a success of almost anything she undertook, in the way of business, or—with a wink at Metabel—in the way of a man, either.

"Oh," said Metabel.

And she sat very still and thoughtful.

She knew what it was to make money—Mrs. Sebold used to make money, in Barly. Mrs. Sebold was a success too: she ran the general store, and was kind to Metabel. But she had never made a success of the fiddler, even after she married him. How did you make a success of a man?

She remembered the words of the little green man: You would like him to be a successful woodchopper.

And all at once she felt strange, as though she had a power she'd never known about, a power which had to do with her being a girl and Joseph's not. . . . It was a smart feeling, her cheeks grew pink, and she took a deep breath; but then, just as she tried to get a better hold on it, it was gone, and she was only Metabel and not a smart woman after all.

But the sun was so yellow-hot, and the air so full of sweet smells, and soft on her face, and the light so gentle and glowing on the earth, that by the time the farm wagon, rattling down the road, drew along into Wayne, she had forgotten all about it.

"There's the Deakan home," said Uncle Henry, pointing with his whip to a large, square house, set behind lilac trees, and painted a neat white. "That's where they live. I wouldn't mind living there myself, though I wouldn't want to leave the farm. But Joseph, now—the farm's no place for him. That's the house for Joseph."

Metabel opened her eyes wide; she looked at the house, then she looked at Uncle Henry. "Whatever would he do there, Uncle Henry?" she asked.

He put his whip slowly back in the whip-socket. "Well," he replied evasively, "I'm not saying. . . . The trouble with Joseph is, he's lackadaisical. He never did seem to stir up any, like other folks. That wood of his—it don't amount to a row of beans. Two trees a week. . . . It's a grief to me. And no ash whatever."

And as Metabel said nothing, only sat and looked at him with a faint trouble in her eyes, he went on to remark that of all ways of stirring up a man from being lackadaisical, the surest way of all was for a good woman to take hold of him. "You take Joseph's mother," he

said, "and my sister: she was a great one for
it. My brother-in-law, Joseph's father, never
did have much ambition till she got hold of
him. He used to carve boats out of wood, to
put in glass bottles. Well, a year after she
took him, she had him building houses. Yes,
ma'am, barns and houses you could live in.
One day he fell off a roof, and landed on a hay
fork. He never did get over it. She was a
great one for stirring people up—one of the
greatest.

"Take Prissy Deakan," he said: "there's another one. She'd get the trifling out of a man.
A man needs a woman now and then to give
him reason to work for. Not me, thank God,
I've got my lettuce."

And as he drew up in front of the bank, he
added over his shoulder, "She has an eye for
him, or I'm a sinner."

He went into the bank with a serious air,

hitching up his trousers held by strings, and looking around him in an important but uneasy way. "Where's your pa?" he said to Deakan's daughter; and went off to discuss matters with the banker.

Prissy Deakan had an eye for Joseph, but it was not a young eye. For one thing, she was no longer young herself; she had a sly, secret look, as though she were saying I kept it to myself, you didn't get it. She was a virgin, a little dry, but able; there was no nonsense about her. "Sit down," she said to Metabel, "and make yourself comfortable." So saying, she turned back to her desk on which lay bills of exchange, bank statements, and other important documents.

Metabel did not wish to admire this older woman who had an eye for Joseph. She would have liked to go past her with her head in the air, and an elegant look on her face. But in-

72

stead, she felt like a little turnip. And she watched with humble pain and admiration the flourishes Miss Deakan made with a pencil on the bank statements.

"There's roses out on Hemlock," she said at last, shyly; "wild ones, in the woods. It'll be a big berry year."

And as Prissy did not reply, she added with a swallow,

"I expect you're too busy to bother."

"Bother?" said Prissy, looking up with a frown; "you mean over berry bushes? I like berries, child; I put up twelve dozen jars last year. That's not counting tomatoes and vegetables, or applesauce. Five dozen raspberries, twenty-four gooseberries, three dozen huckleberries, and a dozen each blueberries and currants. I put them up myself. But large jars, very large jars."

"Oh," said Metabel.

"My . . .

"Well, that's a lot of berries."

Prissy shrugged her shoulders. "What I do," she said simply, "I do so it's done. I cooked myself dark red in the face over those berries. We still have half of them left. This year I'll put up fifteen dozen. Father likes them."

And with a determined look, she returned to her figures.

Metabel sat still, overcome with respect for Prissy Deakan, who knew what she had to do, and did it so it was done. Her own spirit, no more ferocious than a butterfly, felt crushed; she was unhappy; all those jams and jellies weighed upon her heart. She sat humming a little tune to herself under her breath, and staring dismally out of the window, to where Musket stood talking to another dog. She wished she were out there with him, in the sun.

Musket was talking to a young female

74

named Susan who belonged to the banker St. John Deakan. Beneath the legs of Isaiah who towered above them, they were discussing the fact that they had never met before, a fact which exasperated Susan who was accustomed to having her own way. "No," she exclaimed, "this is too absurd. What an amusing time we might have had if only I had known you were here. As it is, I do not find any one to talk to, because no one here is the least bit interesting. I am very fond of stimulating conversation. What fun it will be to go for long walks together, in the fields, or in the woods, where it is quieter . . ."

Musket looked at her with a superior expression. "I am much older than you," he remarked, "and I cannot run about the way I used to. I live up on a hill, and rarely come to town; it is a life which satisfies me, as a matter of fact. When I was young . . . but that is quite another story. I was a dancer. I traveled all over, and I received a great deal of applause. But now, at my age, I must think of the most sensible thing."

"So," she exclaimed with shining eyes, "you are an artist. However, I knew that you were distinguished the moment I saw you. I also do not go about very much; I like older people, because they are interesting. I should like to hear more about your life. A dancer . . . that is most unusual."

"Would you care to see me do a few steps?" asked Musket; and getting up on his hind legs, he began to waltz around very slowly, with an expression of anxiety. Presently he fell down. "Ah," he said; "well . . . at my age, the most sensible thing . . ."

"That was charming," said Susan quickly. "It had a good deal of spirit. What satisfaction you must have from your art. I have often imagined what it would be like to dance; but I fear that I am too clumsy.

"However, perhaps if you were very patient with me . . . after all, I am willing to learn, and I am young."

"Hum," said Musket with a serious look, "that is the trouble. The life of an artist . . . have you any idea of what that means? I should not like to lead you into trouble."

The young female gave a sniff. "Well, really," she exclaimed, "what a surprising thing to say. I confess, I am accustomed to very different speeches. I wonder if I quite understand you. Do you expect me to fall in love with you—is that what you mean? But you are not as attractive as all that, my friend."

Musket moved uncomfortably beneath Isaiah's immobile hoofs. "Do not be vexed," he murmured, "you are really very nice. But I am obliged to be practical. I do not say that you would exactly fall in love with me; why should I think of such a thing? Still you might; it has happened before. What would be the good of it, seeing that I live so far away? At my age . . . well, as I say, I cannot run about the way I used to. No, no, my youth is over. What I want now is peace. Let us forget all this. Do not think about me."

"I see," said Susan slowly, "you are convinced that you would not by any chance fall in love with me. It would be I, not you? . . . That is a novel idea. Set your mind at rest, my friend, I do not find you in the least attractive. I admire your mind, and I would like to talk to you sometimes; that is all there is to it. But I am very busy socially: I go out a great deal, I have hardly a moment to myself. However, if you come to town again, perhaps we can have a quiet talk—that is, unless you are

afraid, or unwilling. I should not like to interfere with your peace up there on the hill. No,
no—go back to your farm and forget me. Forgive me for having spoken to you. . . ."

So saying, she walked away with a sweet
and penitent expression, and a gentle swaying
of the body. Musket looked after her with
chagrin. "Look here," he burst out to Isaiah,
"was I right, or was I wrong? You cannot be
fair to women, they take advantage of you.
One would think it was I, not she, who had
made the advances. It makes me very irri-
tated."

"You are a fool," said Isaiah in his deep
and melancholy voice. "You have talked yourself into something with your heroics. Now
she will give you no rest. It is the finish of
you. She will pursue you, because you have
made yourself out unwilling."

"Do you think so?" asked Musket happily.

And he gazed after Susan with a speculative air.

However, at that moment Uncle Henry and Metabel came out of the bank, and climbed into the wagon again, to go home. Isaiah lifted his head, Musket leaped up behind, and off they went, with a creak and a rattle. But this time Metabel sat silent, with cloudy eyes; and Musket, instead of looking forward at Isaiah, stared dreamily back at Wayne as it disappeared behind them. Only Uncle Henry was talkative, and in the best of spirits.

"Yes, ma'am," he said, "we've got the county bank."

CHAPTER 7

IN WHICH METABEL PLAITS A DAISY CHAIN

"Here is the very home
Of peace, if only you will
Love me a little. Come
There is sun over this hill,
There is quiet under these trees.
Who sings? Only the birds.
Who speaks? Only the bees.
Such tiny words—
Be still!"

sang Metabel, plaiting a chain of daisies to
hang around her neck. The tall flowers nodded
about her; the little wild-strawberry blossoms
lay hidden among them, in the young sweet-
smelling clover where the bees climbed and
sang. The warm air was full of pine scents, the
drowsy fragrance of summer, the somnolent

morning-peace of earth. Her voice, thin as a flute and no more silver, disputed for a moment with the crows who in a distant field settled upon the grain with tuneless cries.

It was not Joseph to whom Metabel was singing; she would have said that she was singing to no one at all, or to anybody. It was a song the fiddler had taught her long ago in Barly, while he was still a hired man, and before he had married Mrs. Sebold, for whom he worked. "There is too much talk in the world," he had said, "and not enough music." He had not played for her to dance that day, because he wished to develop the subject at greater length.

And Metabel agreed with him. "Talk," she had said, "is never as friendly as looks." She thought of it now, sitting in the daisies, weaving a daisy chain. Her young heart beat with joy for the bright sun and the warm earth, for

its flowery fields and friendly-looking skies.
She put out her arms as though to take it all
to her breast: there was no end to it, no end to
sun and blossom, to lazy hum of bees, no
end to youth, the heart's shy hope, the sweet
swift longing, like singing and cryin*g* together
. . . for nothing at all. . . .

Oh, to do for somebody, to care for somebody. . . .

Joseph came through the daisies, tall and
dark against the sun. She waved her hand to
him, full of flowers. "Joseph," she cried. But
then, suddenly, sitting so low among the
daisies, and having to look up so high to him,
she turned shy again. "Did you see Musket
anywhere?" she asked. And she added in a
bright voice, "Do you know what I'm going to
cook for your supper? Mushrooms."

"Ah," said Joseph. He sat down beside her,
looking quiet and pleased: he seemed to be

saying to himself, It is a very fine thing to have mushrooms.

"Uncle Henry likes them," he said as though it couldn't be for any one else she meant them.

But Metabel had already retreated into some happy silence of her own, as though, with him sitting there beside her, there were time and time enough to talk, to-morrow, maybe, or the week after. . . .

"Musket's up to the house," he said, "setting on the door-step, looking down the hill."

And he added, curling his long legs under him,

"He's got a trouble on his mind."

She nodded her head soberly. "Yes, he has," she agreed. "He's solemn as a bee.

"What do you think it is, Joseph?"

"Maybe it's just getting old," he said. "Sometimes it takes you like a trouble. And then again, sometimes it takes you solemn.

"And sometimes," he concluded, "it takes you sort of hand-in-glove with God Almighty."

"Isn't it the truth?" she said. "You take our preacher down to Barly, the Reverend Flood. He was the hand-in-glove-with-God-Almightiest-man you ever see. I expect he was going on fifty years old. A powerful preaching man. When I fell down a cistern my pa dug, and broke my leg, he gave me a book with pictures of martyrs being eat by lions. It brought on the shivers."

"Ah," said Joseph comfortably.

"He was always figuring to make me over godlier," said Metabel sadly.

"Ah," said Joseph again. And he added kindly, "Well, that's it; somebody always wants you different."

"I expect they do," said Metabel, swinging her daisy chain up and down in front of her. Suddenly she burst out: "Joseph I can't bear being changed over. Folks always want you like they are themselves. Seems like they couldn't be happy otherwise, or else call you queer . . . can't a body be queer by herself without being lonesome? I wouldn't care to change so much as a mouse's tail."

"No," said Joseph.

"Aren't you ever lonesome, Joseph? Because I am . . ."

But that was beyond Joseph's simple thought. "What for would I be?" he asked.

"Not for anybody?" She looked down, her lashes veiled her eyes, dreamy and demure. She was minded to say, not for Prissy Deakan? But the slight flutter of her hands swinging the daisies was the nearest she came to it.

He put out his own big hand, brown and horny, to touch her knee. "I know," he said, "you're thinking of your pa." And he remained reverently silent.

86

She gave a tiny sigh, wholly in disbelief. "I expect I was," she agreed.

"Would you ever go to live in town, Joseph?"

"What for would I?"

"Oh," she said vaguely, "to get along, or to see somebody."

"I get along all right up here," he answered uneasily.

"I know you do. But to see somebody?"

He stared at her with a frown. "Who would I want to see?" he asked in an anxious voice.

"Oh—somebody." The daisy chain swung up and down harder than ever. "Prissy Deakan."

Prissy Deaken . . . why, yes, he'd go to town to see her, on business at the mill, or with his uncle to the bank. She glanced up at him swiftly, but his sober, puzzled gaze told her nothing. Did he know that Prissy had an eye for him? He never showed it, if he did. Maybe he didn't mind; maybe he felt, despite himself, the power of all those jams and jellies. What if he admired her, too . . . ? Very well, then.

"There was a boy in Barly," she declared, "I used to know. Lemuel Watson. He could play on the piano."

"Yes," said Joseph politely.

She considered a moment, while the daisies swung slower and slower. "There were a lot of boys in Barly," she continued. "My friends," she explained. That was a lie: it almost stuck for good in her throat, and never got out at all.

"It's nice to have friends," said Joseph.

"Yes, it is," said Metabel. She seemed to be picking her way here and there among words: it was almost like a dance, with the little feet of her mind going one two three hop. But the

88

dance wasn't right yet; it wasn't smooth and lovely.

"We went to school together," she said: "Lemuel and me."

Joseph sighed. "I never did go much to school," he remarked. "All that book-learning . . ." And he sighed again, oppressed by the weight of all there was to know and think of in the world.

But Metabel was not to be jogged from what she was after. "You take Tiny Flood," she insisted, "the preacher's son. He was a caution. Do you know what he did? He tried to kiss you at dances."

"No," said Joseph.

"Well, he did," said Metabel. "Didn't get him anything, though."

"I'm glad of that," said Joseph grimly.

The daisy chain was quiet now, on the ground. But deep inside, where nobody could see, she was dancing free and lively. Should she go on, she wondered, about Tiny? What an elegant liar she was, to be sure. For shame, Metabel; who ever tried to kiss you at a dance, or anywhere else, for that matter? But she knew one thing—that Joseph didn't like to think of it.

She could stop dancing now, she guessed, and pluck a daisy's petals.

He loves me, he loves me not . . .

"What does it say, Metabel?"

"Well, . . . guess."

He shook his head. "How would I guess," he asked, "not knowing? This man in Barly, now—this what's-his-name Watson."

She giggled then. "Oh," she said, "him."

And she turned happily back to the daisy petals.

He loves me not, he loves me . . .

The pines took the sun, broke it down

through green needles, laid it in flakes of yellow and green on the forest floor. In the meadows among the clover the bees went on climbing and singing, meeting and re-meeting each other with brief, inaudible greetings. The sweet warm scent of daisies hung like a morning mist above the ground; the young summer danced and sang. Joseph was glad Tiny Flood hadn't kissed her.

He loves me . . .

"Come along," she said, "let's look for mushrooms."

CHAPTER 8

IN WHICH METABEL LEARNS THAT A SMALL
GOD'S LIFE IS NOT AN EASY ONE

SHE was walking home through the woods,
holding out her skirt full of mushrooms, when
she saw the little green man again. He was
bending over, peering anxiously into a spider
web, in which a young grasshopper, lustily
kicking, was being covered with death-shrouds
by the spider, preparatory to the first good
bite.

"You are just in time," said the little man,
pointing to the web. "I am horrified by this
tragedy," he exclaimed, "in which I am un-
able to help either the spider, or the grasshopper. One must not try to defy the laws of

nature; it is not for nothing that spiders are not vegetarians. If I were to meddle here, the spider would die of starvation. Nevertheless, the struggles of the grasshopper fill me with a sort of woe. What do you think of it?"

Metabel did not reply; seizing a twig, she freed the captive, and watched the spider flee for her life along the broken rafters of her home.

The little green man shook his head disapprovingly. "Now see what you have done," he said. And he added unhappily, "Ak, the hungry spider."

"I like grasshoppers," said Metabel, "better than spiders."

"You are a silly girl," said the little man; "you ought not to interfere in the lives of creatures about whom you know nothing. The spider is much more useful than the grasshopper. She is tidy, serious, and optimistic."

"Still," said Metabel loftily, "I like grass-hoppers better."

So saying she started off through the woods in the direction of the cottage.

The little green man trotted along beside her. "How is Joseph?" he inquired. "You have been picking mushrooms; you are going to cook him a fine mushroom stew. Ah, um." And he gave a deep sigh.

"I am only a silly girl," said Metabel, "and I don't know anything about how Joseph is. I suspect he's all right, thank you."

She walked along rapidly, her head in the air; her stride, awkward but dignified, caused several of the mushrooms to tumble from her skirt held out like a basket. The little man picked them up for her.

"Why are you in such a hurry," he asked, "when you have really nowhere to go? If you do not know how Joseph is, it is useless to ask you. . . . I will wait and ask Miss Deakan when she comes."

Metabel stood stock-still; and more mushrooms fell out. "Is she coming here?" she asked; "here, on the hill?"

He replied that the Deakans sometimes came to supper at the farm.

"Oh," said Metabel in a small voice. "Well," she added, in a voice smaller still, "why not?" And she started forward again, faster than ever. But after a while she slowed down to a dawdle.

"I like Prissy Deakan," she said at last, defiantly.

"Hum," said the little man.

"Anyway," Metabel insisted, "I think she's very nice."

The little man looked at her with a wry smile. "Why do you try to fool me?" he asked. "Do you think I do not know the terror which so much vigor and so many jellies inspire in your heart? You are afraid of her, my child, and so am I, because she would like to make a success of Joseph. She loves him for what he will be when she gets through with him. But you and I love him as he is."

"Do I?" asked Metabel.

The little man shrugged his shoulders. "Such questions," he said, "are not important. You will find out for yourself, when the time comes. Then I will tell you what to do. In the meanwhile, you are about to cook him a mushroom stew. Nothing could be nicer."

By this time they had come to a grove of ash trees, whose paler trunks now stood above them straight and tall in the green forest light, while silver leaves showered them with shadow and shine. The little green man stopped and looked about him in a benevolent way. "Here is my home," he said: "this green and quiet

grove. Here, among these trees which Joseph
loves, there is no one to dispute with me."

Metabel looked up at the trees which
seemed to look gravely back at her. "It's
lovely here," she said. "It's like what I
thought."

The little man continued, musing: "Yes, his
heart is like the woods, fertile and friendly.
There everything grows, for no other reason
than that nature is generous, and does not
make distinctions. But Uncle Henry's heart
is like a bed of lettuces, grown for a prize. In
that dry brown earth there is no room for me.
He would like to turn my home into cords of
wood."

He smiled at her, and again she thought
how friendly he looked, friendlier than Joseph
even. "You are here to help me," he said,
"you are here to keep these woods quiet and
green. Perhaps I even brought you here,

against your will; for the gods must be ingenious if they wish to get along in the world: a god must be a little sly in dealing with other gods, particularly if they are bigger than he is. I am small, but I am sly and stubborn; for that matter, nothing is so obstinate as good humor.

"Well, it is necessary, I can tell you; for the life of a god is not an easy one. For one thing, he is not immortal. Men's faiths, for which they would like to die, or kill one another, do not last very long; in a thousand years, they are forgotten again. Nevertheless, what wars are waged in Heaven in the meanwhile, to the accompaniment of thunder and lightning.

"But here, on this hill"—he rubbed his little hands together—"here in these quiet woods, I can walk up and down day after day, all by myself, without being jostled by Weights and

Measures, or battered by the wings of Methodist Angels."

"O my," said Metabel piously; and she glanced up with anxious gray eyes past the tree-tops to where she expected Heaven was, in case it looked dark and indignant. But the sky beyond the leaves shone just as blue as before.

"Well," she said uncertainly, "I don't know. . . ."

Holding her skirt before her like a basket, she walked soberly home through the woods, followed by a mouse who wished to speak to Musket.

There she set herself to wash and cut the mushrooms. She stood at the kitchen sink; her thin hands dipped like tiny swallows into the pot and out again. But her eyes remained dreamy and confused, her thoughts far away. She thought of what the little man had said:

99

"Perhaps I even brought you here against your will." Was she to do battle with the monstrous Prissy Deakan? Her heart beat with excitement. First of all she would have to get over her feelings of terror and respect. And then . . . what? The little man had said he would help her; but what help was he? Not even to a grasshopper in a web. And she saw herself, a tiny David, opposing without weapons the armored Goliath. "I'll just take up my sling shot," she said to herself, "and haul back, and let her have it."

She went through the motions, with a mushroom for a pebble. "Bing," she said to Musket, launching her vegetable into the air.

Musket was enchanted. "She is dancing," he thought; "this is like old times." And he hurried out, to find Isaiah, who had just come back from town.

100

CHAPTER 9

IN WHICH MUSKET DISCUSSES MARRIAGE WITH A MOUSE

HE FOUND his friend in the barn, still standing patiently between the shafts of the wagon.

"Well," he said to him after they had exchanged greetings, "what is the news from Wayne? Come, let me hear some gossip: I am sure you have heard something amusing."

Isaiah looked down upon him in surprise. "Why should I hear any gossip?" he asked. "What do you expect? The Stebbins' cow has calved. But surely that is not what you wished to hear?"

"Yes, yes," said Musket, trying to be hearty, "that is very interesting. But it is not exactly what I had in mind. I thought perhaps . . . some social bit . . . well, tell me, were you at the bank?"

"Aha," exclaimed Isaiah, "so that is where the wind blows. Yes, I was at the bank. I saw your little friend Susan, also; she appeared to be enjoying herself, and in the best of health." His voice dropped to a graver note. "She was not alone, my friend."

"Why should she be alone?" asked Musket easily; "I hardly expected she would be. She has many friends. So she was enjoying herself; that is a good thing. I should not like her to be unhappy on my account." He gave a deep sigh. "After all," he said, "I am not young any more. The best thing for me is a quiet place like this, where there is nothing to do."

"She was not even thinking of you," said Isaiah.

Musket replied irrelevantly: "The thing I like about her is that she is intelligent. Do you remember how interested she was in my travels? Also the fact that I was an artist appealed to her."

"Well," said Isaiah kindly, "it appeals to her no longer. You told her to forget you, and she has done so. What are you anxious about?"

"It is not always easy to forget people," said Musket in a gloomy voice.

"Nonsense," said Isaiah; "a lot of exercise, or good hard work, and the thing is done. There is nothing like getting up a sweat, to take the mind off its troubles. But do not worry about Susan, because I doubt if she was as much attracted to you as you imagine. From what I saw yesterday at the bank, I should say that she was something of a flirt." And he gave a chuckle like a low whinny.

"Ah," said Musket thoughtfully, "women: there's a strange thing for you. One never knows what to expect. They are like you, Isaiah, always looking in the distance. All a woman wants is to want something.

"Did she say nothing about me at all?

"Very well," he concluded; "one makes up one's mind, and then what happens? Some one else, who has also made up his mind, comes out ahead. But what of it? One must be a little philosophic about such things."

And he moved away with an enigmatic expression. Suddenly a mouse ran out of a hole and gave him a sharp bite in the leg, at the same time exclaiming, "Excuse me; I took this means of attracting your attention."

With a polite look, the mouse added, "I am engaged to be married. However, my thoughts are all at sea. Marriage is not what it used to be; I do not know my way about any more.

What do you think? You have had so much experience."

"Not," said Musket thoughtfully, "with marriage. But it is true that I have thought a great deal about such matters. What is it you would like to know, my friend? However, first tell me: is this a marriage of convenience, or the result of passion?"

"Alas," said the mouse, "I do not know." His voice sank. "My fiancée," he murmured, "is not a virgin. She has already been unfaithful to a number of my friends. Nevertheless, to be near her fills me with rapture. But I am obliged to admit, it will be more convenient for her than for me."

"Women," said Musket in a noble manner, "are unfaithful by instinct, inclination, and the force of circumstances. So do not let that trouble you. I remember once when I was dancing in a little town . . ."

"Yes, yes," said the mouse hastily; "but what about me?"

Musket looked down at him with a superior expression. "Well, tell me," he said, "why do you wish to marry her?"

"Because," said the mouse, "she wishes to settle down in a respectable way. She says that she knows what she knows, and that life is not all what-you-may-call-it. As for me— God help me; I love her.

"However, should I marry her? That is where I would like to hear your opinion. I do not understand these modern ways."

Musket replied musingly, "She has had experience; and she believes that life is not all what-you-may-call-it. She would make you an excellent wife, my friend. As for what she knows, that would only make her more intelligent. For one thing, she has learned that vigor without wit is of no use to her. I congratulate you."

"You mean," said the mouse dizzily, "that it is I who am the fortunate one? You think, then, that I should go on with this?"

"At once," said Musket, "before the lady, who believes that life is not all what-you-may-call-it, changes her mind. Marry her, my friend, but do not believe her. Enjoy yourself as much as though you were not married at all."

"Thank you," said the mouse. "This is very helpful." And he ran off through the grass in a dazzled way. Musket heard him calling, "Elizabeth, I have something to say to you."

Isaiah, who had been listening to this conversation, exclaimed sternly:

"Musket, you are a scoundrel."

"Isaiah," replied Musket firmly, "you are

going at it from the wrong end. I am not a
scoundrel; I am simply on the side of the wife.
Well, look here: she expects love to be lofty.
She is married; and her virtuous husband at-
tacks her with appetite and embarrassment.
By the time he is ready to go to sleep, she is
sunk in despair. Phoo, what a ridiculous thing.
That is because there is some attempt to be
pure. If it were a sin, they would enjoy themselves.

"Women should sin a little before they are
married, for the joy and the experience."

"No," said Isaiah; "you are a scoundrel,
that is all there is to it."

Musket shrugged his shoulders. "After all,"
he said, "you have spent your life on a hill.
And much of it has been, as you say, devoted
to perspiration. I have not been a dancer for
nothing; I know what I know. It is the
woman who is not ashamed to love. Left to

herself, she would make heaven out of such things. Unfortunately, she has been kept in the background."

"That is the place for her," declared Isaiah.

He added uneasily, "I do not like this sort of talk, it makes me very uncomfortable." And he looked around, to see if there were any females within hearing.

Musket looked up at his friend, who towered gloomy and surprised above him. "You are an old fogey," he said. And he trotted off in the direction of the kitchen, as Uncle Henry came into the barn to rub the gray horse down.

CHAPTER 10

MUSKET MAKES A SENTIMENTAL JOURNEY

THAT evening Musket sat a long time on the door-step before the house. The blue dusk deepened about him, the stars came out in the sky like frosty lights. Behind him, in the warm kitchen, in the yellow lamp-glow, Metabel stood dishing out mushroom stew to Joseph and Uncle Henry. "The best mushroom stew," said Uncle Henry, "I ever eat." But Musket did not care. Around him in the darkening air trembled the voices of his friends; the crickets sang, and the cicada, the tree-frogs creaked *kreef kreedn kreedn* . . . voices of earth in the warm sweet night, voices of love, lonely and longing. . . .

The last light faded from the sky, the lamp in the cottage was extinguished. New stars arose, the crickets hushed their song. The night poured like a slow wind over the earth, and vanished in the west; the dew of morning, silvery and cold, fell upon the little dog who lay with his nose on his paws before the kitchen door. He shivered in his sleep, and woke and yawned.

Shaking himself, he walked across the yard, lifting his paws above the dew puddles, stretching himself in the gray morning light. He was hungry and cold; he wished he were snug in bed with Metabel. He stood a while, dejected and uncertain, before the barn, where he could hear Isaiah moving in his stall. "I am a fine one," he thought, "at my age, to stay out all night. In the morning my bones ache." But when the red sun rose, and all the earth grew warm again, he felt more gay. No one was up: the gray horse was still in the barn. If he were to go for a little walk, no one would ask him where he was going. . . .

The birds were waking, their voices skipped and sang among the leaves. The whole earth seemed to stir with joy, to give forth sweet odors, to quiver with happy sounds. Musket's heart beat with pleasure. "What a morning," he said aloud, "to be going for a walk. Supposing one were to meet some one one were fond of . . . a lover's meeting on a summer morning. Ah well, such things have happened to me before."

A beetle who was going by replied pensively, "Why do you wish to meet any one? For every meeting, you can look forward to a parting. The same two who are so irresistibly drawn to each other to-day, will be just as irresistibly drawn apart to-morrow. Life hurries them by on other business, often tearing

112

off a leg or a claw which has become too inextricably entangled. No, no, my friend; go alone, I say."

"I was not speaking to you," said Musket; "however, I thank you for your friendly interest. As you see, I am alone; nor am I apt, I imagine, at my age, to find a companion. I simply thought I would take a walk—a stroll in this delightful air. Down-hill is the way to go. But I do not expect to go as far as Wayne."

"Enjoy yourself," said the beetle, waving a claw at him. A moment later, with one claw still in the air, he stumbled over a twig, and fell upon his back, where he lay, looking at the sky. "When one is alone," he reflected, "one does not have to consider the safety of a second party. Life and death are often no more than a twig apart. What an undignified difference." And feeling already in his body the talons of some hungry ants, he closed his eyes to the inevitable.

Musket continued on his way, heedless of the groans of the unhappy beetle. When he came to the first turn in the road, he thought he would go a little further, in case there were anything to be seen down there. . . . There was another turn, which he took for the same reason. He felt happy without knowing exactly why; he was excited, but he did not wish to ask himself for what reason. However, when he had come within a mile or so of Wayne without meeting any one on the road, his spirits began to sink, and he moved more slowly. "It is too early," he thought, "for any one to be up.

"What did I come all this way for?"

But just as he was about to turn back, he caught sight of a small brown figure trotting along the road in his direction. His heart gave

114

a thump; and he remained as though paralyzed. Then, with an awkward motion, he went forward to meet her. It was Susan.

"Just imagine," he murmured, "finding you here."

"Yes," she said, "how strange. I was out for a little walk. . . ." And they stood regarding each other with shy looks.

Presently Musket turned his head away, in order to let Susan examine him more closely. When she had finished she also stood erect, in a favorable position, and delicately looked aside while he regarded her. Then without a word, they started up the road together in the direction of the farm.

Susan was the first to speak. "I am glad to see you," she said simply. "I have thought a great deal about you."

"Indeed?" said Musket. He spoke in a low voice, so as to conceal the fact that he was pleased and confused. He felt wary; nevertheless his heart seemed to grow larger. He bent upon Susan a friendly eye. "You have been happy?" he asked.

"Happy?" she replied slowly: "yes and no. I do not lead a very interesting life. For the most part, I am alone."

"You were not alone yesterday," said Musket mildly.

She gave him a glance of surprise. "No," she admitted; and looked away. She seemed to be changing her mind about something. "No," she continued brightly, "I was not alone. Indeed, far from it." She gave a light laugh. "Do you know with whom I spent the afternoon? He is supposed to be irresistible."

"Ah," said Musket; "so he is that sort. Well—did you find him irresistible?"

And he awaited her answer with anxiety.

She did not reply at once, but went to the side of the road to examine a fungus. Then she came back again with a languid expression. "To tell you the truth," she said, "I do not like to have proposals made to me so soon, or with such assurance."

Musket was conscious of a disagreeable sensation in his stomach. "He must be a very impudent fellow," he exclaimed.

"He is not unattractive," said Susan, "although for my taste, personally . . . the truth is that he has had too much attention. He does not care for any one but me, he said. Of course, I do not take all that very seriously. For instance, I do not believe that he lost his heart to me really . . . he simply found me sympathetic, because I let him talk about himself."

"Yes, yes," said Musket. And he added, under his breath, "Do you expect me to believe you?" But it did not help him to think that Susan was a flirt; he seemed to himself to grow more unhappy than ever.

"Come," he thought; "pull yourself together.

"Sympathy," he said, "is a very dangerous thing: like pity, it looks to be more than it is. Then you find that certain things begin to be taken for granted. It can be very embarrassing. Once when I was dancing in a little town . . ."

"Exactly," said Susan; "but one cannot change one's nature; if one is naturally sympathetic and friendly, there is no use trying to be anything else. Besides, it makes life more agreeable. Of course, one is apt to be misunderstood; but so far, I have never had any trouble. As for my friend last night—I admit, he was a little forward. I do not like to have things taken for granted."

118

"I hope that you were very short with him," said Musket.

"No," said Susan, "why should I be? He knew that he would not be allowed to presume. . . . After all, there is no harm in talking. I like to be gay in my talk, and a little intimate. For one thing I feel that it is expected of me. But I can assure you, I said nothing which might have made him think he had a right . . ."

Musket replied dryly, "One does not make proposals unless one has first been allowed to hope. If he insulted you, it was because you let him think that it would please you, and that your answer might be yes."

Susan gave a gasp. "That is absurd," she said. "Besides, I did not say that he insulted me."

"It is not absurd," answered Musket gloomily. "He made you proposals; they surprised you. That is what is absurd, as a matter of fact; because you know very well what to expect."

She stood stock-still, and looked at him with indignation. "It is you who insult me," she said. "I wonder why? What right have you to say those things to me? First you tell me not to think of you—as though that were all I had to do. . . . Well, that was insulting enough, or would have been, if it weren't so ridiculous. And now you say that I know what to expect. No, really, I would rather walk alone, if you please; I came out to enjoy myself."

"So did I," replied Musket. "I came out for a pleasant walk. Instead, the entire time, I am obliged to listen to some proposals a stranger made to you. Of course, it is nothing to me. But I cannot help seeing it in its true light. First you lead him on; then you complain. Probably you are very cruel."

"At least," said Susan stormily, "I am not cruel to you, because you can leave me at any minute, and go back where you came from. You are perfectly free; so why do you vex yourself by staying in my company? I am quite able to get home alone, thank you."

Musket gave a shrug. "Or you in mine?" he asked. "Besides," he added, "if you will notice, I am actually on my way home."

"You are insufferable," said Susan; "it is really too bad, because I thought, when I met you, that I liked you. I thought that you were intelligent, and kind. But you are like all the rest, stupid and conceited."

"I am not," said Musket angrily. Then, growing more dignified, he added, "I too, thought that you were different. But you are like the others, vain and untruthful. I am glad I am not your lover."

121

"I would not have you for my lover," said Susan, "for anything in the world."

"It makes me happy to think," said Musket, "that you are nothing to me."

"Or you to me," said Susan.

"Fortunately," said Musket, "I live so far away that we are not even apt to meet each other very often."

"Fortunately indeed," said Susan.

With these words she turned around, and started back to Wayne. When she had gone about a hundred yards, she looked back over her shoulder and remarked, "I am not cruel at all."

Musket did not hear her because at that moment he was exclaiming in a loud voice:

"I am not conceited."

CHAPTER 11

RAIN ON HEMLOCK

"What do you think about good humor, Uncle Henry?" asked Metabel.

"Haven't I got it?" said Uncle Henry.

Rain had settled over Hemlock; gray cloud tatters trailed on the mountain, the air was searching, cold and sweet. Icy drops fell from the trees on to the bushes; in the drenched garden Uncle Henry was taking this last opportunity to thin out his lettuces.

Metabel stood beside him in a rubber cape, the hood up over her head. The cape was too long for her, it came to below her feet, and lay in the puddles. The thrum of the rain was in her ears as it moved, driven by the wind, across the fields and through the woods; it made her want to dance, but when she put up her arms, cold trickles of water fell down her neck. So she stood still and peered anxiously across the garden to the black sopping woods, where the little green man lived.

"I wonder is he comfortable?" she thought.

Uncle Henry, with an oilskin over his red flannel shirt, knelt on the ground. "Haven't I got good humor?" he asked. "I always figured I had. Look at the way I go after these lettuces, rain or shine; and what thanks do I get? But I don't complain. Look at the way I am with Joseph: there's good humor for you. Here's a head for the table. It's got a spot on it."

And he held out to her a lettuce soaked with rain. She put it under her cape.

"I don't think that's what he meant," she said thoughtfully.

124

"What who meant?" asked Uncle Henry.

"Nothing," she said; "I was just thinking."

"You do a powerful lot of thinking," complained Uncle Henry, "and what with the dancing you do, you're liable to waste most of your life.

"Like Joseph," he added gloomily. "He has the whole side of a mountain to lumber, and what does he bring out of it?"

"Neat cut wood," said Metabel. It popped out of her mouth, to her own surprise.

"I wouldn't give you two cents for it," said Uncle Henry. He pointed to the lettuce. "There's my prize head," he said. "When they see that, they'll know who's living on Hemlock. There's not much bigger grown."

Metabel gave the lettuce a polite look. "I like the little ones best," she confessed. "They taste sweeter."

"For eating," agreed Uncle Henry, "for

125

eating. But I'm not raising lettuce for eating
I don't care for them myself. It's a work with
me. I don't like it, but I do it. Do you know
who gets the good of it?"

"No," said Metabel honestly.

"The county," said Uncle Henry, "the
county gets the good of it. Wayne County
where they grow lettuces as big as a barn
Folks hear of that. And I'm the one up on
Hemlock, in Wayne County, that grows it
It's a way I have with vegetables. But the
county gets the good of it. And why do I do
it? Because I've got an opinion of my fellow
men. I've got an opinion of myself. I'm a help
to this county.

"Take Joseph, now." And he prepared to
continue this subject which vexed and per-
plexed him.

"He has no opinion," he said sadly. "It's a
grief to me."

126

"But wait till a good woman takes ahold."
And he rubbed his wet hands together, thinking of what was going to happen to Joseph.

"I know what you mean," said Metabel.

"That's it," he said cheerfully; "that's the
one for him. She'll take hold of him good. No
more setting and thinking for Joseph. No
more neat cut wood for him.

"I can see it in her eye. Last time I was at
the bank she said to me, 'How is Joseph?'
'Come to dinner,' I told her, 'and see for yourself.' 'I will,' says she. There's a woman for
you: 'I will,' she said, just like that."

Metabel looked out across the rain-soaked
fields with startled eyes. It gave her a turn,
his saying that; it made her feel as though
there weren't so much time ahead as she
thought. Time had always seemed something
infinite to her, stretching out ahead of her, full
of lovely things—all she had to do was to find

127

them, and then live happily ever after. Eve
after, for always and always. But this wa
different: something was trying to happe
which would change everything. Time wasn
infinite, it was moving very fast, it was comin
to an end. . . .

Her breath caught in a sudden panic. If i
happened, the thing which was trying to hap
pen, then there'd be no loveliness ahead an
more. She didn't stop to think—she simpl
knew. One couldn't just take one's time abou
things—one had to do them quickly—shar
and sudden—I will, or I won't, just like that
That was the giant one had to face with n
more than a sling shot—not Prissy Deakar
Well, she'd face him, in whatever panic, an
let him have it.

Remembering what she had seen in Barly
in the Book, she exclaimed, "He fell upon hi
face to the earth."

"Who?" asked Uncle Henry. "Not Joseph?"

"No," said Metabel, "not Joseph."

And she tramped off through the wet grass to the barn, already fragrant with clover-hay, her long rubber cape making a trailing whisper as she went.

In the barn she found Joseph, sewing an old harness for Isaiah. He smiled when he saw her. "Hello, Metabel," he said, "I was thinking about you."

She stood still, taking the cape down from her shoulders. "Were you?" she asked, hardly believing it. "What were you thinking?"

He replied seriously, "I was thinking were you happy here?"

"Oh," she said. She looked at him with eyes gray as the rain outside. "Don't you know, Joseph?" she asked quietly.

No, he didn't rightly know. "I always think

129

folks are happy," he said musingly, "till I stop
to think. Then I think maybe not. It's a
queer thing, happiness. I expect it's not the
same for everybody. I declare to God, you
might just as well let them be.

"Don't you ever wish yourself home again?
Tell me true."

Metabel wanted to say No, right out. But
then she stopped; the little sly part of her got
up inside and looked around. The rain fell
with the wind against the barn in a long sweet
whisper. Barly . . . Barly . . . why did Joseph care?

"Who's in Barly," she asked, "would want
me back?"

"The preacher's son?"

She smiled to herself. He hadn't forgotten
that much, at any rate. "Well, he might," she
said, lying. "But I don't mind staying."

Joseph looked earnestly at the harness in his

hands. "I'm right glad to hear it," he said. "It wouldn't be the same hereabouts, if you went. Uncle Henry's got that used to you."

Uncle Henry? Was that all? "Not you too, Joseph?"

"Yes . . . too. But I mightn't always be here."

Her heart went down with a swoop. "You're figuring on going away?" she asked, looking at her feet, and trying to keep her voice from trembling.

He wouldn't look up, either. His voice sounded trifling—too trifling, almost. "I don't know," he said; "I don't exactly aim to. But Uncle Henry keeps pestering me; he wants for me to go down to work at the mill. Winters."

He gave a sigh. "I guess maybe I'm just no-account," he said anxiously.

Again she bit her tongue to keep back the No which started coming out fit to break its neck for speed. What was it kept her from saying the thing she wanted to say? It was almost as though she were set to give herself a hurt if she could. "You'd be right near to Prissy Deakan," she said, "if you went to town."

"I would, too," he admitted.

She stood looking at him for a long while. Then, slowly, and with a shiver, she put her wet cape on again. "Why don't you go?" she said. And turning on her heel, she marched out of the barn into the rain.

It cooled her face, it made her pulse go slow again. The cold, wet air steadied her, started her thoughts to going orderly. Whatever was she up to, marching out like that? He hadn't said he'd go—he hadn't even said he wanted to go. There she was; she'd met Goliath, or at least had a look at him; and what had she done? Run away the first crack out of the box. Hadn't even stayed long enough to sling one stone. "Glory," she thought, "we've got each other all mixed up."

And suddenly she seemed to see the little green man at her side again. "Where's your good humor?" he was saying to her. "Nothing is so obstinate as good humor."

She took a deep breath of the sweet, searching air: it stung her nose. "All right," she said aloud. And back she went to the barn again.

"Joseph," she said, "do you want to go to Wayne?"

He shook his head. "No," he said. "I declare, I don't."

"Then don't go," she said. And with a firm, peaceful expression, she sat herself down next to him, and took over her share of the sewing.

CHAPTER 12

THE DEAKANS COME TO DINNER

But that didn't keep the Deakans from coming to dinner. All three of them, St. John the banker, Prissy, and Susan, came up in the Deakan automobile one hot summer day, drawing the dust behind them. Uncle Henry and Joseph met them at the road, all in their Sunday best: over the faded red flannel, Uncle Henry had buttoned a blue and white checked cotton shirt, which Metabel had carefully washed and ironed; while Joseph, with his hair wetted down until it shone, had got himself into a corduroy jacket, hot but elegant.

Metabel herself was nearly distracted, what with the cooking she was expected to do, and

the looks she wanted to give herself—not that
she had more than a ribbon or two to add between her worst and her best, but even the
ribbon, she felt, ought to take fixing. She was
all for the cooking and letting the looks go,
until she saw Joseph's shiny face and wet-
down hair; then she was all for the ribbon. It
gave her a hot feeling in her heart to see him
getting himself up so grand for any one else.

She stopped before her little mirror, and
gave herself a long, disdainful look. "You're
an ugly piece," she said, "and what good's a
ribbon going to do? You might as well tie it
on to Musket; all you've got is an old dress,
anyhow, with holes in it." So saying, and with
a dreamy air, she arranged the ribbon at her
shoulder, and pinned it on with a black safety
pin. Then she turned around, and gave a skip
on her toes. "How do I look, Musket?" she
cried.

Musket did not reply. He seemed excited, and at the same time his thoughts were elsewhere. He trotted to the door, and looked out; then he came in again, and sat down in a corner. But in a moment or two he was back at the door again, peering down the road with an uncertain expression which he hoped would be taken for indifference.

Metabel turned back to the mirror, and gazed at herself with falling spirits. Then she gave a sigh. "Oh well," she said, "I don't care." And she went back to her pots on the stove, from which the steam presently wilted the ribbon until it drooped like a shoestring.

It made no difference, for the moment Prissy came in, she felt like a little humble toad again. Prissy in her store clothes, looking large and cool and able—looking as though she knew more about cooking than Metabel, more about lettuces than Uncle Henry . . . but not, Metabel, thought with a quiver, more about cutting down trees, quiet and neat, than Joseph did, thank heaven. . . .

"We had to bring Susan," said Prissy; "she came running after us, and wouldn't be left. I'm glad to be here; it's cooler than the valley." And she looked around the room in an ample way. "There's been changes," she said.

Her eyes fastened on Metabel, bending anxiously over the stove. "That's right," she said; "I forgot you had a hired cook."

Uncle Henry brought a chair forward for the banker. "Sit down, St. John," he said, "and ease yourself."

St. John eased his large spare body into the chair, and mopped his face. "It's hot, Henry," he complained. "There's like to be thunder by night. It'll sour the milk." He exhaled a long breath; it was his habit to talk about things like milk while his mind was going over figures. He believed in being strong inside, and amiable out; it took a little longer to make an impression, but it made it deeper. After he had been amiable for a while he'd bring out his figures, and strike other people, who had no figures, dumb. Uncle Henry was used to it; as soon as the banker started talking about milk, Uncle Henry began to think in terms of acres and lumber. He'd be ready when the time came.

"Yes, sir," he said proudly; "thunder up here is the loudest in the state."

Musket and Susan stood together in the doorway, looking out across the yard. "Isn't it funny, my being here," said Susan; "will you believe it, they insisted on my coming. As a rule, the woods do not attract me. However, there was no help for it to-day."

These words did not fool Musket, who wished to say, "You were obliged to come, but not for the reasons you have given me." Nevertheless, he held his tongue, content for the moment with his advantage. "I am glad you came," he said gallantly, "even against your will."

Susan looked at him out of one eye. "Perhaps it was not wholly against my will," she murmured. And as Musket said nothing, she added in a faint voice, "It is so hot in here; shall we go out?"

"Why do you dislike the woods?" asked Musket as they trotted down the steps. "They are cool and quiet and green; the little moths fly about in the half-light; there are caves under the rocks, and houses under fallen trees. It is just the place to be on such a hot day. Besides, you are not likely to be disturbed. It is very peaceful."

"What an alluring picture," said Susan. "As a matter of fact, I do not dislike the woods.

139

Some unforgettable things have happened to me there. . . . I suppose that you have some little place of your own to which you usually go; a soft carpet of moss, a hidden hollow with the sound of water falling, green branches overhead making a sweet half-light . . . you see, I am not unfamiliar with the woods. Of course, you would naturally know of such a place."

"Yes, indeed," replied Musket; "I am most anxious for you to see it. Let us go a little faster; then there will be more time afterwards."

"What a romantic creature you are," said Susan. And as they disappeared among the trees, she was saying, "I like things to be made a little attractive. The brutality so in vogue to-day does not appeal to me."

At dinner Metabel did the serving, sitting down to eat with the family, and hopping up again to fetch things from the stove. Her hair was wet and stringy, her thin face red with work; the wilted ribbon on her shoulder hung without dignity from the black safety pin. And Joseph sat there, saying little, with the same friendly smile for Prissy Deakan that he had for everybody.

"If only," thought Metabel, "even once, he'd look as if he didn't like her."

But not Joseph; he continued to look as though he liked everything and everybody. On the other hand, when Prissy looked at Joseph, her eyes grew secret and hard, just as though she were looking at what belonged to her, and having a sly thought about it.

And the worst of it was, there didn't seem to be anything for Metabel to do, except to go on hopping after the dishes. After all, she wasn't David; she couldn't just sail up to her foe and let her have it in the forehead. Prissy looked so sure and able; maybe he did belong to her.

She grew hotter and hotter, her face turned redder and redder; and Uncle Henry and St. John Deakan discussed politics.

"We could send this road right over the hill," said the banker, "if we had more dairy interests. This is a dairy state, Henry. You'd ought to raise cows."

"It may be a dairy state," said Uncle Henry firmly, "but it's a vegetable county. This road has always gone down. What for would it go up?"

"Up and over," said the banker. "A road right over Hemlock. New roads, new farms; bring the wood down. There's a lot of lumber on Hemlock."

"We could use a little more mountain ash down to the mill," said Prissy.

Joseph seemed not to hear. "They want

142

some ash down to the mill, Joseph," said Uncle Henry in a wheedling voice. "There's a lot of it up above us."

"There is," said Joseph. "But you can't reach it."

"They'd give a price for it at the mill," said Uncle Henry.

"Ah," said Joseph.

"We could put a road right up the hill," said St. John, "and bring the wood out. Instead of being obliged to go around by East Toby, like we are now. Ash is what we want. You'd have a tidy property, Henry. A road's a good thing, too, for coming and going."

"There's nowhere I want to go," said Joseph.

"You've no opinion," said Uncle Henry angrily. "Never did have. For all the time you set and think, where's your opinion?"

"That's right," said Joseph amiably.

143

"*Joseph,*" cried Metabel, inside her heart.

"I don't like to take out mountain ash," said Joseph quietly. He didn't seem to be arguing about it; he just said it.

Metabel took a deep breath. "He has his own opinion," she said out loud, "and that's enough for anybody."

At once it seemed to her that she heard a sound of handclapping, very small and faint, just outside the window. Inside the kitchen, every one stopped talking and stared at her. Only Joseph himself seemed unmoved by the declaration. "I expect you're right, Metabel," he said. It made her want to shake him, out of vexation.

"Everybody has an opinion, miss," said Prissy coolly. "Some folks do well with theirs, and others don't. Some folks live in rags"— her hard secret look swept over Metabel's small figure—"and others don't."

144

"That's it," said Uncle Henry; "that's saying something. Do you hear, Joseph? Rags for some, and riches for others. Take your choice."

"What riches," said the banker in his slow voice, "will you ever get out of lettuce, Henry? Cows are the thing. And a proper road for lumber."

Uncle Henry's face grew solemn. "It's my lettuce draws the farmers, St. John," he said. "The county gets the riches from what I do. I get my own riches.

"But that don't let Joseph out," he added gloomily. "You take your axe, Joseph, and go up and have a look at that ash above us. Prissy'll go along with you. I declare, I'm sick of your fancies. St. John, you come with me; if there's to be a road over Hemlock, I want to see."

He went out, to figure cords of wood, to

show the banker his lettuces, to follow the
road in his mind up the hill and over. Joseph
and Prissy went off to the barn, to get an axe.
And Metabel took her dishes to the sink, and
got the suds ready. As a rule she enjoyed
washing up, the warm water, the bright, shiny
china in stacks on the table; but now she had
no patience at all. Her thin fingers flew and
stumbled; she felt all of a hurry, as though
she had no time for what she had to do. She
pressed her wet hair away from her face with
the back of her hand. A road up Hemlock, and
the trees down? Her heart gave a flutter of
fear. And why did Prissy look at him like
that? Was there something between them?
She had an eye for him . . . she certainly had
an eye for him.

"There never were so many dishes," she
cried, "in the whole world. Oh, go on—get
clean, for goodness' sake. . . ."

CHAPTER 13

A STORM IS GATHERING

HEAVY heat lay on the hillside that afternoon, heat almost as heavy as a mist. The
birds were still, even the crows forgot to caw;
only a locust stung the silence with the drill
of his sound. At the wood's edge Metabel
came upon Musket; the little dog's head was
hanging, and he dragged his feet wearily.
Susan walked beside him; she took mincing
steps, and gazed at him in a hopeful way.
But Musket did not return her glances. When
he passed Metabel, he hung his head lower
than ever. Finally his legs collapsed, and he
sat down. "Ak," he said. "Yoo. My legs are
not what they used to be."

Susan wished to console him. "Never mind," she said; "I am not sad about this, really. Supposing that in the future we simply confine ourselves to conversation? Come, cheer up; life is not all what-you-may-call-it."

Musket gave her a startled glance. Then he closed his eyes with a groan. He did not feel consoled at all.

Metabel went across the dry grass into the woods. There it was more silent still: the green leaves, dusty with heat, closed behind her, and drowsy shadows peered at her from out the tree trunks. Dark, gloomy, the trees gazed down at her; and again she felt the need to hurry, as though something were pushing her. Was it the trees, pushing her? They were so very still. There was something queer about them; the very silence itself, up there among the branches, seemed to be thinking a strange thought. Or was it a fear? Yes—it

was more like a fear. The forest was afraid.
It made her feel scary.

"Little green man," she whispered; "little
green man . . ."

But no one answered; and the silence grew
deeper. A dry twig broke under her feet with
a pop; she began to run. "Wait a minute,"
she said to something; "wait . . . I'm coming . . ."

The faster she ran, the more frightened she
felt. It seemed to her as though the forest
were running with her, as though shadows
skipped along behind her and about her, from
tree to tree. *Pat pat pat* went her feet, but all
she could hear was the sound of silence, like a
great hum. She closed her eyes. "Wait," she
cried; "oh, please . . ." Her foot went under
a root, and down she came with all the world's
pain in her ankle.

When she opened her eyes, she found herself buried in a sumac bush, at the edge of a little clearing into which Joseph and Prissy were at that moment slowly walking. In the center of this clearing stood a great ash tree, toward which Prissy was directing her steps.

"Ah," said the banker's daughter, "that's a tree. Look how straight it is, Joseph. Like the mast of a ship. A tree like that would bring money at the mill."

"Would it?" said Joseph, without enthusiasm.

Prissy laid a hand on his arm. "Joseph," she said seriously, "I want to talk to you. I'm right fond of you. You know that."

"I like you too, Prissy," replied Joseph.

Her face grew pink, the eyes softer, then harder. "I'd like to see you get along," she said.

"I do get along," said Joseph; "I get along fine, Prissy."

She spoke a little impatiently. "Yes," she said; "but that's not what I mean. I'd like them to say about you down to the town, 'He's a good man.'"

"Don't they?" asked Joseph with surprise.

She turned and looked at him honestly. "No," she said, "they don't. And you know why, Joseph? They say you're no good with a tree, and that's the truth of it."

Joseph looked unhappily at his axe. "It pleases me, the way I cut," he said. "I cut slow, but the tree goes where I want it. I've taken out a chestnut between two birch, and never cracked a limb on either of them. That's the way I like to cut, Prissy. What's the matter with that?"

"It don't get you anything," said Prissy. "It don't get you cordage. That's what we count at the mill. Not what you leave, but what you bring out."

Her fingers twined on his arm. "Joseph," she said in a low voice, "bring me a load of ash to-morrow."

"I don't want to, Prissy."

She looked at him, all softness and wheedle for a big woman. "Start on this one, Joseph," she said. "Bring it down for me.

"Bring it down fast and neat. I've never seen you cut."

In her sumac bush, Metabel, with one hand on her ankle, and her mouth screwed tight with pain, was looking for a stone. "God give me a stone," she said to herself.

"Who's that called my name?" asked Joseph.

Prissy glanced around in surprise. "Nobody," she said; "there's no one about. I didn't hear anything."

Joseph looked at the tree and sighed. "I'll bring you down an oak, Prissy," he said coaxingly; "that's a lot better than an ash. I can cut fast if I've a mind to. It's only that I've never had a mind to. A fine stiff oak. You'll see."

"The mill's full of oak," said Prissy wearily. "What we need is ash. This would be just for me, Joseph. You said you liked me."

"I do like you, Prissy. But you're asking me to go against what I've a mind for."

"Then you're plain no good with a tree. That's what they say in town. Well, they're right."

"They're not either," said Joseph. And he advanced slowly but angrily to the tree.

"Look here," he said, turning around, "somebody threw a stone at me."

"You're crazy," said Prissy, with a gasp; "go on—begin. Let's see you cut. Let's see you . . . if you can."

Up went the axe, and down it came on the

tree, which gave a groan. In her sumac bush, Metabel closed her eyes; her heart was going like a little trip-hammer. Goliath had his big knee on her. "Help," she croaked, inside herself.

"I don't want it to fall on that sumac over yonder," said Joseph chopping away.

"Faster," cried Prissy, "faster . . . "

"I can't get direction so good when I'm going fast," puffed Joseph.

"It doesn't matter," cried Prissy. "Faster, Joseph . . . oh . . . "

The tree creaked and cracked; the upper branches shivered, the leaves gave one last desperate dance, and down it came with a swoop and a roar—square on the sumac bush.

"There you are," said Joseph. "I didn't get my direction very good. Do you want me to chop it up here and now?"

But Prissy was satisfied; her face was pale,

she looked languid, almost drowsy; when she spoke, her voice was thick and sweet, like molasses. "No," she said, "come home." And she took his arm. As they moved off, her legs seemed to wobble under her.

The fall of the great ash had flattened Metabel out like a little pancake. It came down on her like a wave, all rushing and roaring; she didn't feel anything, the thunder and the fear seemed to blot out all feeling. She gave one faint cry, "Oh, pa . . . " and closed her eyes. For all she knew, she was dead; broken to pieces. It was the end of her.

In the quiet after echoes, she looked around again with eyes all ready to brim over with pain. But it was queer, the pain held off; nothing hurt her, except her ankle. Was she numb? Was she so smashed she couldn't even feel pain? She looked anxiously for blood, or broken bones, but nothing was broken or bloody. "Oh," she said with a groan, "ow." And she waited wide-eyed to see if anything ached.

But nothing did. Instead, a voice at her ear exclaimed, "What are you groaning for?"

There at her side was the little green man.

"Now look," she cried; "just see what's happened."

And she explained earnestly, "A tree fell on me."

"I know it," he said.

Then she saw that he was holding up one of the branches in such a way as to make a sort of shelter over her. He did not seem in the least vexed or uneasy; as a matter of fact, he was smiling.

"I could have died," she said; "I could have been smashed to kindling."

"Yes," he replied; and then, "nonsense."

She looked at him for a long time, while her

rain-gray eyes grew darker and darker. Finally she pointed a trembly finger at him. "You did it," she said. "You made it fall on me."

He nodded his head. "I did," he admitted.

"Well," she gasped, "I never. What on earth for?"

He did not reply. Instead, he looked thoughtfully up at the sky. "The hot spell is broken," he said. "Soon there will be a storm. Thunder on Hemlock is the loudest in the world."

And as he spoke she heard above her in the tree-tops, a heavy sough of wind.

"I'm going home," she declared.

At this the little green man looked anxious and gloomy. "No," he exclaimed hurriedly, "that is impossible. A tree has fallen on you."

"But it didn't hurt me any," cried Metabel.

"That makes no difference," he said. He

added earnestly, "What do you think I did all this for! It is not a pleasure for me, exactly, holding up this tree. . . . But what an opportunity. Go home indeed—no, no, my child, that would spoil everything. Supposing it is a little uncomfortable for you; never mind, it is a time for courage. One does not win battles by going home at a critical moment. Do you know what is going to happen? In the morning Joseph will come to look for you; led by Musket, he will find you under this tree, which he cut down against his will, for Prissy's sake. What a night he will spend, looking for you. And what a morning, when he has found you. O my. That is the end of the road up Hemlock."

"But," objected Metabel, "that isn't fair for Joseph. I'm not hurt; I could crawl home easy."

"Think how much nicer it will be," said the

158

little green man cunningly, "to have him carry you home, all anxious for what he has done to you. And once you are in his arms . . . well, hum. Now do not argue any more, but make yourself comfortable. While we wait, I will tell you some stories. What would you like to hear? I remember everything."

"You're so obstinate," said Metabel beginning to sniffle; "I hate you. I don't want to hear stories, I want to go home."

The little green man gave a chuckle.

"Nothing is so obstinate as good humor," he said. And settling back with a contented sigh, he began: "Once upon a time . . ."

CHAPTER 14

THUNDER AND LIGHTNING

THE light faded ominously with the day, leaving the woods in darkness hidden from the stars. The wind increased; sighing, it passed overhead, among the leaves, which rustled in the air. Thunder rumbled up from the west; at last, between flashes of lightning, the rain came rushing over the tree-tops with a marching sound. The upper branches bent beneath that rush of water. But at the foot of the trees, the drops fell with a loud, hesitant patter, their solid fall broken and scattered by the leaves.

The little man drew down the branches of the tumbled ash to make a cover for Metabel;

it did not keep her wholly dry, but it kept off some of the rain. When the lightning broke too brightly through the clinging dark, she closed her eyes and moaned. The little man held her hand and comforted her. "Come," he said coaxingly; "there is nothing to be afraid of. I do not think he really means to hit us. Besides, his aim is poor; he is always hitting the wrong person, and then taking the credit. However, to be sure, I have put a small piece of steel in the branches of a tree a few yards away. Originally it was a mouse-trap. You are safe with me; but do not let go of my hand."

"Do you mean some one's trying to hit us?" cried Metabel. "Ow."

The little green man replied seriously, "The gods are always fighting. I alone have no such desire; and that is what makes me unique. I do not even urge my rabbits to attack Uncle Henry's lettuces. What is the good of quarreling? But the gods do not feel amiably inclined toward those who will not fight with them. Accustomed to arguments and battles to prove that the other gods do not exist, they cannot bear a mind in which there is neither envy nor disapproval. Like you, I have almost no friends in Heaven, because I do not wish to fight about anything. That is what attracts me to you."

"I wanted to fight about Prissy," said Metabel soberly, "but a tree fell on me."

"That is different," said the little man. However he did not explain how it was different. He continued: "While their mortal admirers slaughter each other upon earth, Heaven resounds with divine slaps and blows. The god of the Jews has had his nose pulled many times. But he is tough; almost as tough as I am. I respect him for his obstinacy. I would like to be friends with him, but he will not have it. 'There is no good humor,' he assures me proudly, 'among the Jews.' And he covers up his beard with his hands, to keep an enraged Baptist saint from pulling it out."

"I didn't know it was like that in Heaven," said Metabel.

At that moment a blinding flash of lightning, attracted by the mouse-trap, lit up the forest like day.

Metabel sat up with a start, shivering from fright, and from the cold water which fell on her from the trees. "I want to go home," she said.

Letting go of the little man's hand, she exclaimed with energy:

"Why did I ever leave Barly?"

The little man seemed to dwindle at her side. "If you go on like that," he said, "I shall soon be too small to hold up this tree any

163

longer. Then you will be squashed for fair. Or Satan will get in here, and throw me out. He is very ugly; if he knows you are frightened, he will come at once. Already I hear his wings in the dark; my nose detects an unmistakable odor of sulphur and molasses. Give me your hand; hold on to me tightly."

And he exclaimed in a loud voice, "Go away, Satan; nobody wants you. We are all brave as lions here."

"All right," said Metabel in a tiny voice, "I won't be scared. Don't leave me." And she held his hand as tightly as she could.

They were silent; the trees dripped down on them, the storm rode sullenly off into the east, banging and blazing. The girl closed her eyes and dozed; when she woke, the little green man was stirring uncomfortably.

"It is nearly day," he said, "and I have a crick in my arm. In a few minutes the sky

164

will begin to turn gray, and cocks will crow in the villages. Soon Joseph will be coming through the woods crying 'Metabel, Metabel.' It is time for me to leave you, my child. I have arranged a stick to hold up the tree until he gets here.

"But before I go let me give you some advice. You are in a very favorable position. Do not bungle this opportunity. When Joseph arrives, act a little hurt; weep a little, make some touching moans; if possible, faint. Remember that a tree fell on you; it was his fault, and you have every reason to be upset.

"And think that what you are doing is not entirely for yourself. As a matter of fact, that part of it does not interest me. It is for the woods, it is for me, it is for Joseph himself that you must act wounded this morning. The eyes of many little mice and rabbits are upon you. Farewell."

With that, he was gone. At the same time, the light in the woods turned gray; cocks began to crow; and Metabel heard through the trees the anxious voice of Musket, and Joseph calling, "Metabel, Metabel."

Musket was the first to reach her; he poked his cold nose into her face and jumped about.

When Joseph saw her under the tree, he turned pale. "O heaven," he said. And he began pulling at the tree like a demon.

Metabel gave a melancholy groan. "Joseph," she said faintly, "is that you? A tree fell on me."

Seeing that his back was turned, she gave Musket a sharp slap. "Stop licking my face," she whispered, "for goodness' sake. . . . "

The little dog sat down and stared at her in dismay. "Ai!" he exclaimed.

"I've been here all night," said Metabel in her faintest voice.

"Are you hurt?" cried Joseph. "Are you mangled?"

"I'm mangled," said Metabel. And she closed her eyes, intending to faint. But then she opened them again, thinking she'd put it off for a better time.

"My ankle's swole," she announced.

Dropping to his knees beside her, Joseph exclaimed with anguish, "It was Prissy's doings. I'll never forgive myself, nor her, neither. O Metabel, look what I've done to you."

Now, thought Metabel, was a better time to faint than the other. But before she let herself go limp, she sat up and exclaimed with energy, "You'd never let her do it again, would you, Joseph?"

"Never, so help me," said Joseph fervently. He gathered her up, white and wet in his arms. "Ah," she murmured, "oh." And she acted like fainting as well as she could.

167

Home they went through the gray wet woods; from the dripping branches little squirrels looked down at them with happy faces; mice gazed up at them from under logs green with moss.

"Hurrah for Metabel," they cried.

"She is a noble creature."

Joseph paid no attention to these sounds, which seemed to him like so many squeaks. He held her close and light as a feather; her face rested against his shoulder; it made her heart beat, to feel the rough cloth of his shirt, and the strong arms around her. But after a while his feet began to lag, for he kept looking at her. "No," he said, "I'll never get over this. She's fainted. Metabel. Don't faint. We're nearly home."

So saying, he put his face down next to hers, to make her feel better, probably.

She stretched one thin arm up around his

neck. "Joseph dear," she murmured, able to talk, "you won't let them make you over, will you?"

"No," he said. And he gave her cheek a brave kiss.

"Hum," he added thoughtfully; "well . . ."

Her arm tightened about his neck. "Hold me closer, Joseph," she said, "because I'm wet. I'm mangled, and my ankle's swole. Did you give my cheek a kiss?"

"Yes," he said.

"Oh," said she. She closed her eyes contentedly. "It felt like it," she said.

He brought her home, and set her down in the chair. Uncle Henry gave one look at her, and went for hot water. "I knew you for a fool," he said, "the minute I laid eyes on you; but I didn't figure you for the biggest fool there was. Couldn't you get out from under a tree before it fell on you?" However, when he saw her ankle, blue and swollen, he grew merrier. There was no question about it, it was an important swelling.

While the ankle was being bound, Musket went off to find Isaiah. The little dog's tail drooped, and he looked forlorn. "What a night," he said to the gray horse; "looking here, looking there . . . I was not prepared for it.

"Tell me, why do they try to fool each other? If they feel anything, they should say so, and be done with it. What is all this, hiding under trees, and giving me a slap? . . .

"There is something queer here."

CHAPTER 15

ONE STAR OVER THE PASTURE BARS

UNCLE HENRY went to look at his lettuces for the last time. One more day and it would be too late, they'd go into seed. Already the smaller ones were high in the middle; one or two, even, had a great stalk darting up through the leaves.

Uncle Henry looked at them for a long time. While he gazed and gazed, the sun sank slowly in the west, and a chill stole out of the woods, in the shadows. There, before him, lay his size and his glory, but he felt weary. He was a worshiper, from whom the ecstasy had departed. He had grown those lettuces, teased and coaxed them to be bigger; that was what he loved, raising them. Now that they were grown, something stopped in his mind; he was just so big, they were just so big, and there was nothing more to be done about it. If only the spring held over, and things went on growing. But no; all the great effort of June, and were you any bigger by September? Christmas time you were as small as ever.

Not quite, perhaps—there was the prize up over the fireplace, and farmers from as far as East Toby spoke of those famous vegetables.

Yes, they spoke of him. His bosom swole, but not very much. He wasn't young and hopeful any more, he'd learned how big the heads would grow—so big, and no bigger. What he wanted was a lettuce to go on growing through July and August, through October and November. . . . He sat and thought of other things, things like roads; yes, there wasn't any end to them, you could go on building them bigger and bigger, further and further. . . . Perhaps he should have been a road builder. Perhaps he should.

He drew in a breath; his nose detected the fragrance of Indian pudding from the kitchen. Weary, but consoled, he returned to the house. There, at least, was something couldn't be better.

In the cool evening light Metabel and Joseph stood together by the fence above the pasture where Isaiah, with a faint *clop, clop*, was moving slowly through the grass already wet with dew. Below them, near the woods, the fireflies were darting like little golden sparks into the air cold with the mist of night; while above them, over the dark, still trees, trembled the evening star, white and alone.

His arm was around her, her thrush-colored hair lay against his shoulder. Serious and happy they stared without winking at the

173

green clear sky above the tree-tops. Then
they wished together on the evening star.

> *"Very first star I see to-night,*
> *Wish I may, wish I might . . ."*

Ah, Metabel thought, why not? Here was
the world all full of a light which made it look
so lovely . . . the green twilight from the sky,
perhaps . . . why shouldn't she wish for what
she wanted to come true? There she leaned
in Joseph's arm, with her head against his
shoulder, loving him; and did he love her
back? He had his arm around her, anyhow.
Her heart almost spilled over with happiness.
To be loved, even a little. . . . What a
strange, shy burning it put into her eyes when
she looked at him, across the table, or suddenly coming in through the door. . . . And the
way her heart beat, now and then, all of a sudden, making her want to dance, only that she

didn't know, ever, how to dance as gay and free as her heart felt. She loved him, he had his arm around her, and oh, how sweet the evening smelled. . . .

She blew a kiss into the air. "That's for a little green man who lives in the woods," she explained.

"What a fancy you've got," said Joseph.

"Never mind," she cried gaily. But her mood passed, leaving her solemn and anxious.

"Joseph," she said, "are you glad I came here from Barly?"

His arm tightened about her, but he said nothing; he stood quiet and smiling. He was never much for talk, was Joseph.

She went on, in a low voice, with her head against his shoulder: "I told a lie, I haven't any friends there. There was just the fiddler who ever cared for me. But that was different, too. He didn't put his arm around me. He was an old man."

She looked up at him sweetly. "I guess I always knew I'd be happier some day," she said.

"You and pa would have got along fine."

"Wouldn't we?" agreed Joseph.

"He was no-account," said Metabel humbly, "but he could be smart when he wanted. He used to plug the holes up in my shoes with gum." She took a long quavery breath. "Do you like me, Joseph?" she asked in a tiny voice.

He bent his head. "Yes," he said.

"Better than . . . anybody?"

"Oh . . . better."

"Better than Prissy Deakan?"

"Yes."

"Well," she said as bravely as she could, "I'd marry you if you wanted."

"That's what I aim for," said Joseph simply.

She did not know that her heart had stopped, until it began to beat again. An awful joy took her by the throat. "O my," she said; and she closed her eyes faintly.

After a while she opened them again, on the green sea of the evening sky and the dark shore of the woods. "You're my sweetheart now," she said with solemn wonder.

"Yes," said Joseph, giving her a happy hug.

"I love you," she whispered, but only to herself. She was shy; it was such a thing to say: she tried it over. "I like you," she said.

"I never liked any one before."

The calm and happy night touched her heart with loving fingers; a late last thrush sang in the dusk a few sweet evening notes. How happy, how happy she was . . . and strange to say, how sad; a little wandering grief trembled in her joy like a leaf in the wind. It was nothing, it was too much happiness, it was the night being so beautiful, it was that star shining so bright, it was because she wanted to cry. . . .

"You're crying," exclaimed Joseph, astonished.

She shook her head; two tears rolled down her cheeks. "I'm not," she said.

"It's your pa," said Joseph kindly. "There." And he laid a timid kiss in her hair, like a small bird in a nest.

She turned with a cry, and took him in her arms; thin, eager, they twined around his waist. She buried her head against him, just below his breast, where it came. "I don't need a pa," she cried, "if I have you.

"I don't need anything."

And she looked up at him, her face pale, her eyes wide and dark as water.

Then Joseph surprised himself; he bent

down and kissed her. Her face was cool, her mouth was softer than roses, softer than flowers . . . he stared at her, and she stared back at him.

"I never kissed any one before," she said slowly.

"Me neither," declared Joseph. He brushed his mouth with the back of his hand; he took his arm away from her; he put it back again; and they gazed solemnly at the sky together.

"Ah," they sighed; "hum."

The thrush was still; far off in the valley sounded a tonk of bells as the cows went home to their barns. The cold night air seemed to gather sweetness, a murmur of wind sounded in the trees. Sighing, it touched their cheeks, and passed on to the field where Isaiah stood lost in dreams.

"Is your foot easier?" asked Joseph at last.

"It's still swole a little," she replied.

Arm and arm they returned to the house where Uncle Henry sat sad and thoughtful, gazing at the stove.

But in the forest there was silence; and the ash trees trembled.

CHAPTER 16

IN WHICH THE ASH TREES TREMBLE

WHAT a queer change it made in the world, being in love—or was it being loved did it? It was like having a merry-go-round in her heart, with people going around and around, laughing and gay, and the music playing . . . in the morning she'd jump out of bed with a gasp; and then jump back in again, to be quiet a moment, to feel how happy she was.

She hugged her happiness to her thin breast. Her happiness—innocent, and without end, it trembled around her and before her, sweet as singing, light as dreaming. Life would never change now; she would never be lonely again.

And the woods, her woods, her fields, her

little paths, all gave it back to her again and again, spoke to her in new and friendly accents. They seemed to say to her, "Now you are part of us, now you belong to us. It is only the lover who sees, it is only the beloved who hears. Little sister to the birds, little cousin to the bees, now that you have given your heart, there are no more secrets left. Under your feet and in the air about you throng your sisters and brothers, their tiny bodies making a music of love, of meeting and parting. Under the wings which flutter overhead, beat hearts filled with longing, poignant and mystical. It is the longing which fills your own heart; it is the pain which makes your eyes so bright, it is the joy which makes your steps so slow."

When she passed a beetle crawling through the grass, she stopped and said to him, "Can I help you? Where would you like to go?"

And she admired his shiny coat and ferocious expression. Her heart was full of kindness because she was in love.

"Go on," she said to the birds, "sing louder."

She went to dance in the woods by the fallen ash tree, wild roses in her hair. She hummed to herself, she floated over the moss . . . one, two, and turn, one, two, and skip . . . but in the middle of it she stopped to ponder, to hug her happiness again: is it me, is it Metabel? Joseph's axe clinked in the deep woods; the sun, falling through the leaves, lighted her face, dreamy and pale. Her slender body stood quiet as a tree among the sister birches, rooted to the earth from which the summer fragrance rose upward to her heart.

In the cool shade of the barn she sewed herself a wedding dress; it was of cotton, yellow and faded. Musket sat at her side, his black, weary head in her lap. "Musket," she said, between stitches, "do you remember how I used to wake up in Barly, in my little room, and look out of the window, and say, 'It's day on Hemlock'? Oh . . . Barly . . . What would the fiddler think if he could see me now? I'll write him a letter, and tell him; the postman must likely know where Barly is; it can't be far.

"I'll say, 'Dear Fiddler, I'm living up on Hemlock Mountain, and I'm going to be married. I'm making myself a yellow wedding dress. We're not going to have a wedding trip, because my husband is not a success. There's a rich girl here called Prissy Deakan, but I slung her with a stone and she fell to earth. Very Sincerely Yours, Metabel Adams.' "

Stitch, went the needle proudly, *stitch.*

"Musket dear," she said after a while, "do you remember my pa? He never was a handsome man like Joseph. He was right smart at gumming up the holes in my shoe, but he wasn't strong, rightly—he was thin and trifling to look at, like me."

Stitch.

She dropped her sewing, and sat gazing quietly at the green fields glowing in the sun. In the cool barn tiny motes of dust swam in a fall of light down through the cobwebbed windows. All was still; she saw a bird go by, and heard, outside, the little hum of summer in the grass.

"Musket," she said soberly, "do you think I'm very trifling looking?

"Poor Joseph, he's not getting much."

She saw Uncle Henry go by, with his brows drawn in a frown. He stopped a moment, put his head in the barn door, to wave at her.

"I'm looking for Joseph," he announced. "I want to show him where a road would go, right up past the north field, if we were minded to build it. Those dairy people, they have all the roads. We'd ought to have one, anyhow . . . a good one."

And he went off again, shaking his head. Already he saw the road he wanted . . . the longest road in the county, it went on and on, nowhere in particular.

Presently Joseph came in from the woods with his axe over his shoulder. Seeing that no one was looking, not even a swallow, they kissed each other shyly; then they sat down together on the feed bin, swung their heels, and gazed at the floor with embarrassment. "What are you sewing?" asked Joseph.

"It's a dress," answered Metabel. "A yellow dress, for being married."

He took it up to look at; his strong brown

fingers felt it and gripped it. He sighed; his feet stopped swinging against the side of the bin. "You'd ought to have a store dress," he said bravely. "I'd ought to buy you a silk."

"Go along," said Metabel; "buy me . . ."

"Well, it's the truth," said Joseph.

Metabel sat silent, while a great wonder spread slowly through her heart. That Joseph should . . . like her . . . was a strange thing; still there it was, thank God for it, it was like a dream, not very real, but how lovely. But this thing about a dress—that was different. That was everyday real. She was going to belong to Joseph, they were going to be one; and he wanted to buy her a dress, the way you would for your own folks. . . . What an amazing moment. Possibly marriage itself would be more astonishing, but it wasn't likely.

"I could as lief make you a shirt out of this,"

187

she said timidly, "instead of a dress for me."

She longed to give him something, too; something of her own. . . . As long as they were one, what did it matter who had the wedding dress?

But Joseph shook his head. His face was clouded; he had it on his mind to buy her something. Not doing it was going to make a difference.

It had only just occurred to him.

He was a poor man.

At their feet Musket was talking to the mouse whom he had advised to get married. "Look here," said the mouse enthusiastically, "how are you? You do not look well. I am very happy, myself. My wife's experience is a constant source of gratification to me. All I have to do is forget where she got it."

Musket replied irritably, "Do not ask me how I am; I am old, and my bones creak.

Nothing is what it used to be, except my folly and my appetite."

"You should find some one with experience," said the mouse happily. "She would make you forget your bones."

"Go away," said Musket, "and do not bother me."

And he went gloomily out of the barn to find Isaiah. When he saw him, he said to him dejectedly, "Are you sure that it was she? It could not have been somebody else? We were to meet in the woods, half-way; she said that she wished to spend the day in quiet conversation. When she did not come . . . you do not think that she was indisposed?"

However, he did not wait for Isaiah's answer, which he already knew by heart. Hanging his head, he went back to the house, and lay down under a chair.

CHAPTER 17

THE ASH TREES FALL

METABEL went on sewing her wedding dress, and Joseph went on chopping wood. But his axe seemed to ring faster, off in the woods; the old, lazy, comfortable chime was gone. He went out earlier, he came home later; and his face, thought Metabel, looked different. It looked sharper, but puzzled. Was he getting opinions, she wondered. He had something on his mind.

One day he said to Uncle Henry, "I'm going up the hill, and have a look at that ash. Maybe I'll send a load of it down to the mill. I could use some money." And he looked at

Metabel as though to say, "We could use it, I mean."

Metabel glanced up in dismay. "The ash?" she exclaimed. "Why, Joseph . . ."

"Well," he said, a little sharply, she thought, "I guess I'm as good a man on ash as the next one."

Uncle Henry looked around with gentle joy. "Ah, Joseph," he said; "ah. Now, then." And he began to think of what he'd say to St. John Deakan about that road. They were going in for lumbering.

But Metabel felt her heart turn over. She followed Joseph out to the barn where he'd gone to sharpen his axe, and took him by the sleeve. "Joseph," she said to him anxiously, "you're never going to cut that ash?"

He looked unhappy, she thought, but stubborn. "I expect I'll have to," he said. "I've got new things to think of now, Metabel."

"You mean about me?"

"Yes," he said. And he added firmly. "I mean to give you what you've a right to."

"Oh," she cried, "but Joseph—if I don't want it?"

"That don't signify," he said. And he said again, "I aim to give you what you've a simple right to."

She stared at him with wide, doleful eyes. Whatever had come over him?

"Joseph," she cried again, as he started off, "where are you going?"

"Don't fret," he said.

But all she could do was fret. In the house again, she went about her tasks with a heavy heart, while Joseph's axe sang on the hill faster and faster, sharper and sharper. Oh, where was the little green man? If the ash trees went . . .

She stopped in the middle of her dishwashing, to wring her hands faintly. If the ash trees went . . .

Would he ever forgive her?

Late in the afternoon a little mouse approached her, and sat up on its bottom. Metabel and the mouse exchanged a long look.

"What do you want, mouse?" asked Metabel.

The mouse did not reply. Instead, he got down on his paws, and started out of the door, with soft backward glances.

Metabel went after him; for she knew who had sent him. Anxiously she followed the mouse through the woods until she came to a clearing where four ash trees lay broken on the ground. On the trunk of the largest sat the little green man, looking very dismal and smaller than ever.

"So," he said. "There you are. Do you see what has happened?"

"Yes," said Metabel unhappily.

"I suppose that you are proud of yourself," said the little green man.

"No," said Metabel, "I'm not." She looked around her at the desolation, the four trees down, their branches tossed along the ground. "He's cut the ash," she said with honest horror.

"He has," cried the little man, "he has. And why? To buy you a wedding dress, that is why. And what do you want a wedding dress for? Ah, you greedy creature."

Metabel stood and looked at him. "So that was it," she said. She shook her head proudly. "I didn't tell him to," she declared. "I was making it myself, out of goods. I didn't want him to cut the ash. I'm not a greedy creature."

The little green man looked at her for a long time in silence. When he spoke at last, his voice was gentle, but sad. "I believe you," he said. "Perhaps you did not ask him to buy you a wedding dress. Still," he added uncertainly, "that is what he wishes to do." And he gazed at her keenly.

To save her life, Metabel could not help thinking, "It's sweet of him to want to." Her heart grew warm; she forgot to be sorry for the trees. But she did not want to admit it. "O dear," she said, like a hypocrite.

The little green man mimicked her. "O dear," he echoed. "But that will not put the trees up again, or keep Joseph from cutting down what is left of them. He is like a crazy man, his axe is like a buzz-saw . . . rip, rip, everything must come down."

"Well," said Metabel firmly, "never mind; I won't let him."

"Ah," said the little green man doubtfully.

"I'll stop him," said Metabel. "I'll tell him I don't want a wedding dress, or anything else.

There—are you satisfied?" And she gave him a sweet smile.

But the little green man was not satisfied; for all at once he got to his feet on the tree-trunk, and leveling a tiny finger at her, exclaimed indignantly, "You—Prissy Deakan."

Metabel stared at him in dismay; then she looked down at herself, to see if she was changed. But she was just the same as always. "Why," she cried, "I'm not."

"Yes you are," he insisted.

"But I'm not," she cried again, "and you know it."

"Well," he said, "you might as well be.

"You've done her work."

"Oh," said Metabel, while an anxious feeling began to take hold of her. Was it more than a wedding dress? What did he mean? The sun was low in the sky, the trees stood about, gloomy and shadowy. Night had en-

tered the woods far away, it was stealing
nearer.

"I haven't done anything," she said again,
in a whisper. And all at once she began to cry.
"Oh, please . . ."

But her tears had no affect on the little
god; his small, divine spirit remained as un-
touched by her grief as it had been unmoved
in the past by her indignation. "Yes," he said
quietly, as though he himself were sure of it
for the first time, "you have done her work,
although you did not intend to. Last night the
gods went through these woods, the Powers
and the Dominations, the Weights and the
Measures. Their heavy feet trod down the
ferns under which mice had taken refuge.
They were laying out roads, they were adding
up lumber, they were dividing these woods
among themselves. When I heard them coming from the valley, I ran away and hid in a

hole under a tree. That was a fortunate thing. Finally I put my head out and said to one of them, 'What are you doing here? Go away.' He did not even stop to answer me. But another one replied, 'It is no longer a question of good humor up here. Joseph is going into the lumber business.' I threw a stone at him, and he gave me a kick. Look."

And he showed her a large lump on his forehead.

"O my goodness," wailed Metabel weeping. "O dear."

The little man went on gently, "Here, in this forest, is my only home. There is no road here, to Milford or Peru; here there are only friendly paths, which return again to where they started, or lose themselves in ferns and shadowy branches. What does it matter that you wish me well, how does it help me that you love it too? Joseph has found a strange duty in his heart, now that he loves you, now that he wishes to marry you. His peace is gone; he longs to be spry and active, for your sake. He aims to give you what he has not got; he will destroy this home to build another, to lay roads, to create a lumber business. You can not stop him, my child, since it is for you he does it. Talk him out of cutting trees? First you must talk him out of loving you."

"Never," said Metabel tearfully.

"I did not think you would say that," remarked the little green man sadly, "although I confess I feared it. What is it that you want? A wedding dress? That is what the neighbors have. Look for it where Uncle Henry sells his lettuces."

"I didn't ask him to buy it," Metabel repeated pitiably. "I didn't want him to."

"No matter," said the little god inexorably, "since he wants to. He wants to take care of you, to do for you as well as any one could. Is that what you want, to be taken care of? To knock down a forest for a wedding dress. . . . O Metabel . . . to steal away his peace of heart to feather your own heart with? Some day he will hate you for it. But first of all you will dislike yourself, my child."

"No," whispered Metabel.

She stood before him, a forlorn, bewildered little figure, clasping and unclasping her hands, the tears wet on her cheeks. Evening was in the woods, the day was gone, only a green dusk lay like moldy light upon the trees. Night was on its way, already it had stolen past the east, it was coming. The woods were silent; it grew darker.

"I will not let you make Joseph over," said the little green man quietly. "I will not let you change him into the likeness of every one else. I have fought for him too long. . . . If I

must turn against you, too, why then I must.
Joseph the successful woodchopper . . .
squeezing the woods, squeezing his heart, to
have what the neighbors have. . . . No, no,
my child, I will never allow it.

"Go back to Barly, Metabel, and leave him
to me."

"I won't," said Metabel.

He shook his head impatiently. "Will you
try to stay in spite of me?" he asked. "Sooner
or later I will throw you out, as I threw out the
other one."

"I thought you were the god of good humor," said Metabel bitterly.

"I am," said the little green man, "but I am
obliged to fight for my home. Already I have
a lump like a toadstool on my head. The ash
trees are down; and trees are down in Joseph's
heart. He does not think of me now, he thinks
only of you. But he will remember me, some

day, when it is too late to find me any more. He will look for me in the lumber business; and when he does not find me there, he will blame you. What will you do then, my child?

"You had better go home now, before it is too late."

Metabel looked at him quietly through her tears. "Must I?" she said. "I haven't anything at home. Here is all I have."

"I will come and visit you sometimes," he said.

He got to his feet; and together they started back through the woods. She could not see very well, it was too dark; but the little green man glowed before her like a firefly, and she followed, dumb and doleful. The trees made a path for them; not even a root rose out of the ground to trip her. The night came stealing up behind her, full of small sounds, dark and whispering. "Oh," she cried, "hurry."

All at once the little green man stood still; and she saw that they had come out of the woods, and were upon a road. "Here," he said gently, "is the road to Barly. It is all downhill. Good-by, my child; I will come and see you some day."

She clutched at him wildly, but already he was gone. "Wait," she cried; "no." Behind her the trees rose like a wall, severe, unyielding. She flung herself back at them, they caught her in their branches.

"Joseph," she cried, "Joseph."

Far off, in the deep woods, a drowsy bird, cheated of his sleep, woke with a cry.

"Joseph . . ."

CHAPTER 18

THERE'S NO ROAD THROUGH

ALL summer long the valleys around Barly are green as the sea. But in autumn they are like yellow pools; over them the clouds swim slowly in the sun, trailing their cold blue shadows across the hills. Goldenrod climbs the slopes, the maples are just turning. How far away the hills look now, touched by the gentle haze of fall, faint, acrid, sweet, like the smoke of a leaf.

It is the time of quiet, the time of crickets and drowsy bees; their voices, faint and sleepy, mingle with the rustle of leaves dying on the branches. Even the blue seems to deepen in the sky, to shine again, as in spring, with other light.

The tassels on the corn were black; the yellow squash, the green cucumbers ripened on the ground. In the window of Mrs. Sebold's general store, the muslin dresses and straw hats were taken down, and corduroys and woolens put out instead. But the bicycle, hard candy, and pocket knives remained as they were.

Once again Metabel sat on the slopes above her little cottage, and watched the red sun rise. Musket was with her; her hand, thin and brown, lay on his head. Her heart was quiet; and her eyes, long dried of tears, searched with dreamy looks for the first beam of day. Her summer was over; she had come home to work for Mrs. Sebold, to dance some day again for the fiddler—not now, but in the spring—to dance, maybe, for more than just the fiddler, in other towns than Barly. . . .

Far in the north Old Hemlock caught the sun; light shone like a fire on its crest. Metabel caught her breath. "Musket," she said, "there's the sun.

"It's day on Hemlock."

Below her in the valley the smoke of Mrs. Sebold's fire rose through the early air, thin and blue, curled at the end like an Indian pipe. And in her heart nodded and whispered the green untroubled woods of Joseph's home, where the sun shone when Barly was in shadow. The forest stood on Hemlock; there was no road through.

Serenely she rose, and returned to her cottage. There, at the door, smiling, stood the little green man.

"Good morning, Metabel," he said.

THE END

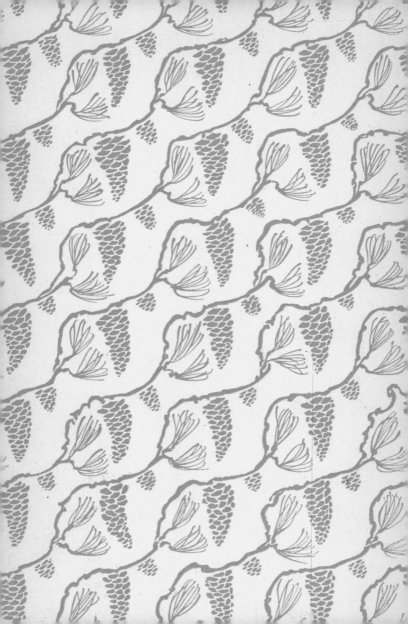